Contents

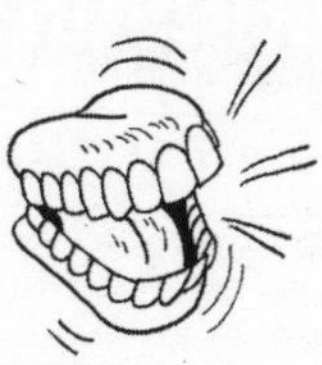

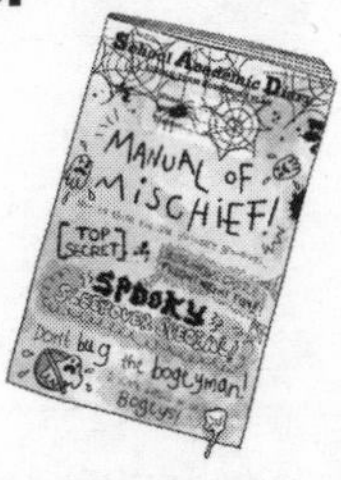
MANUAL OF MISCHIEF!
TOP SECRET
SPOOKY
Don't bug the bogeyman!

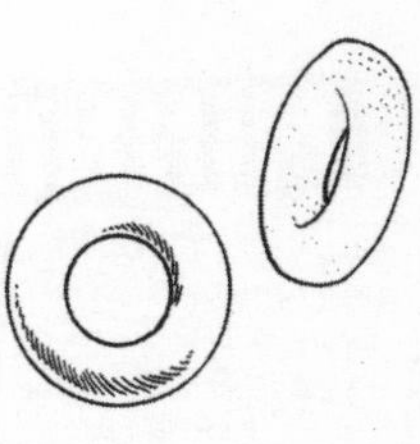

MEET TEAM DENNIS!

If you're reading this **boomic**, you just joined the COOLEST team in the <u>WORLD</u>!

'Book' + 'comic', gettit?

Here are some new friends you're about to meet . . . and some villains you'll want to steer clear of!

DENNIS
BEANOTOWN'S PRANKMASTER–GENERAL!

GNASHER
DENNIS'S AWESOME DOG HAS FEARSOME TEETH THAT CAN SMASH CONCRETE!

MINNIE
DENNIS'S COUSIN, WHO KNOWS THAT SHE'S THE REAL LEADER OF THE TEAM!

PARKINSON
LORD SNOOTY'S BUTLER, PARKINSON HAS WORKED FOR THE BUNKERTON FAMILY FOR MORE YEARS THAN EVEN HE CAN REMEMBER.

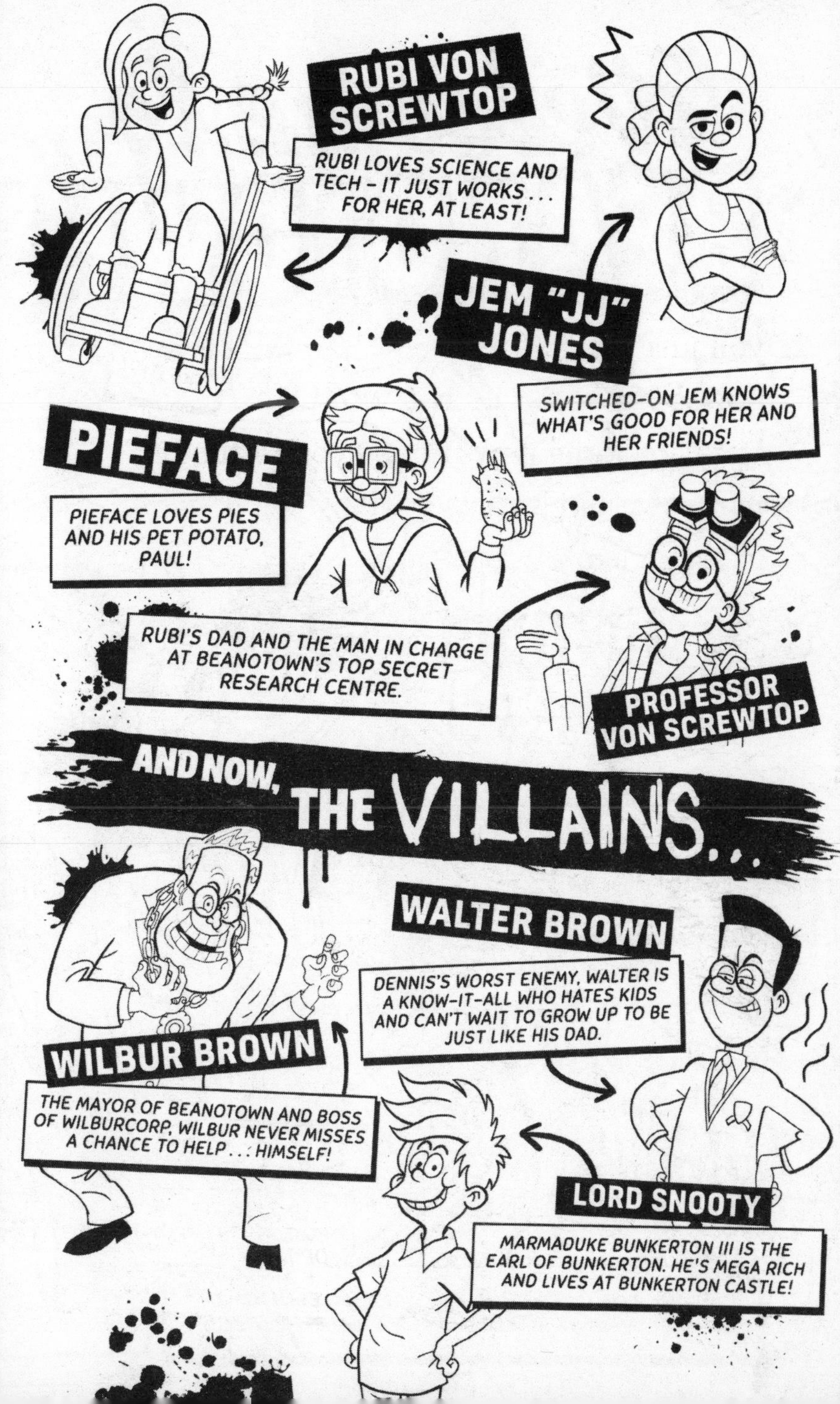
RUBI VON SCREWTOP
RUBI LOVES SCIENCE AND TECH – IT JUST WORKS . . . FOR HER, AT LEAST!
JEM "JJ" JONES
SWITCHED-ON JEM KNOWS WHAT'S GOOD FOR HER AND HER FRIENDS!
PIEFACE
PIEFACE LOVES PIES AND HIS PET POTATO, PAUL!
RUBI'S DAD AND THE MAN IN CHARGE AT BEANOTOWN'S TOP SECRET RESEARCH CENTRE.
PROFESSOR VON SCREWTOP
AND NOW, THE VILLAINS...
WALTER BROWN
DENNIS'S WORST ENEMY, WALTER IS A KNOW-IT-ALL WHO HATES KIDS AND CAN'T WAIT TO GROW UP TO BE JUST LIKE HIS DAD.
WILBUR BROWN
THE MAYOR OF BEANOTOWN AND BOSS OF WILBURCORP, WILBUR NEVER MISSES A CHANCE TO HELP . . . HIMSELF!
LORD SNOOTY
MARMADUKE BUNKERTON III IS THE EARL OF BUNKERTON. HE'S MEGA RICH AND LIVES AT BUNKERTON CASTLE!

Welcome to... BEANOTOWN!

Beanotown Library, Some say it's Beanotown's tallest building – it has the most stories, you see!

This is where the Menace family lives. Menaces by name, Menaces by nature. At least that's what the neighbours say!

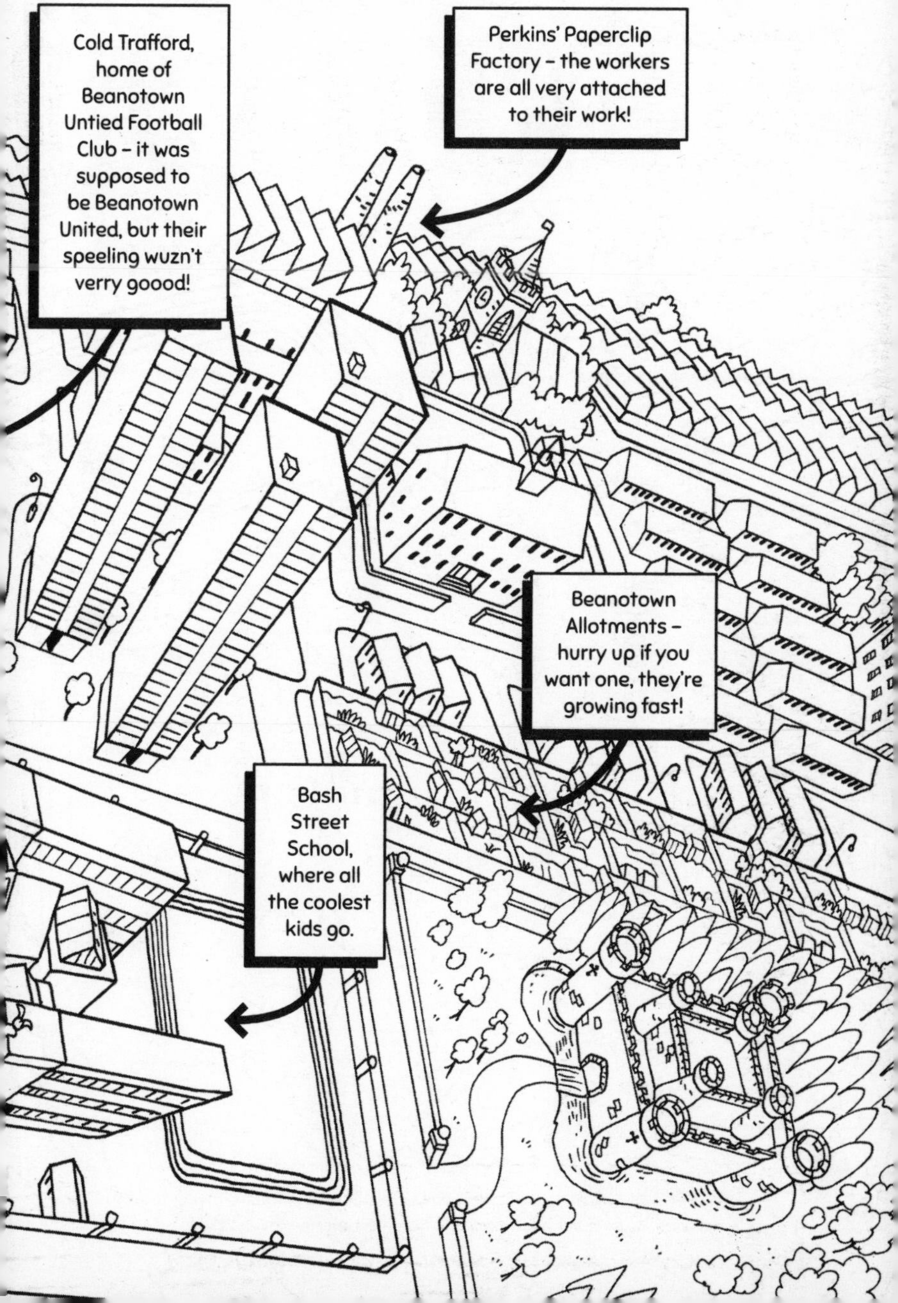
Cold Trafford, home of Beanotown Untied Football Club – it was supposed to be Beanotown United, but their speeling wuzn't very goood!
Perkins' Paperclip Factory – the workers are all very attached to their work!
Beanotown Allotments – hurry up if you want one, they're growing fast!
Bash Street School, where all the coolest kids go.

Chapter One

HASSLE AT THE CASTLE!

Dennis Menace is the kind of kid who thinks doing one thing at a time is lazy. He prefers to do at least three things at once.

Right then, he was doing his homework, cleaning his teeth, and running to school. He was in a hurry because he'd hit the snooze button seventeen times. Mum had got him out of bed eventually by telling him it was Saturday when it wasn't.

And that was just plain mean!

When he got to Bash Street School, his friends were huddled together looking at a newspaper.

'Did you hear about Snooty?' asked Pie Face, who always hated it when people he knew were having a hard time.

'I hope he's OK,' said Jem. Jem knows how important it is to look after yourself and she makes sure her friends don't forget it.

'Snooty will be fine,' said Minnie. 'He's pretty tough . . . almost as tough as me.'

Minnie is Dennis's cousin, and she is genuinely one of the kindest, smartest, coolest, most admired people in the world.

At least, that's what she wrote about herself on her Bash Street School pupil profile.

BASH STREET SCHOOL YEARBOOK

MINNIE MAKEPEACE
I am awesome!

'What's going on with Snooty?' asked Dennis, walking over to his friends.

Pie Face showed him the newspaper's front page.

Snooty is what Dennis and his pals call their friend Marmaduke Bunkerton. Snooty is ten years old and goes to Bash Street School. And he's also a Lord. A proper Lord, like you see on the TV, only younger and not asleep all the time.

Snooty lives at Bunkerton Castle, which is the oldest, grandest building in Beanotown.

It is huge, but the only people who actually live there are Snooty, his Aunt Matilda and Parkinson the butler.

Just then, a gloomy figure sloped into the playground. It was Snooty.

'Hi guys,' he said, a bit wearily. 'I guess you've seen the news?'

'Give us the scoop on the scares, Snoot!' said Minnie. 'What's been going bump in the night at Bunkerton?'

'Go easy, Min!' warned Jem.

'It's all right,' said Snooty, bending to pat Gnasher. Gnasher licked his fingers. 'I guess I always knew this day would come. The Bogeyman of Bunkerton Castle has terrorised my family for generations, and it seems it's out to get me now.'

Dennis, Minnie and Jem felt a chill run down their spines, while Pie Face felt a little gravy run down his chin.

6

'The Bunkerton…Bogeyman?' Pie Face asked.

'It's the curse of the Bunkertons,' sighed Snooty. 'The Bogeyman of Bunkerton Castle has haunted that castle for centuries. I thought it was a silly superstition, but the bogeyman is back!'

'You don't believe that, do you?' asked Minnie incredulously.

'Not at first, but then the noises started.

HORRIBLE MOANS, PIERCING SHRIEKS

and a relentless, DRIP-

DRIP-

DRIP

coming from *inside the walls*.'

'Next came the poltergeist phase. Precious heirlooms mysteriously fell off shelves. Ancient weapons slipped from the wall, missing me or my aunt by millimetres.'

'And now,' Snooty went on, 'the bogeyman visits me every night. Even if I lock my bedroom door, it gets in and screams at me.'

'What does it scream?' asked Jem.

'LEEEEEAVE!' yelled Snooty, making his friends jump. 'LEAVE THIS PLACE FOREVER!' 'Made you jump!' Snooty smiled, but a little sadly.

'The bogeyman has been visiting us for

a month and I've had enough. I'm selling
Bunkerton Castle and moving to the city.
I'm going to open a gallery and share my art
collection with the world. I'm going to see a
nice flat tonight, actually.'

9

'What?! You can't let some bogeyman scare you out of Beanotown!' said Minnie fiercely. 'If you leave, whose butler will I drench with my water blaster?'

'And what about your friends?' asked Jem. 'Won't you be lonely?'

'I'll make new friends,' said Snooty, 'but you can all come and visit me anyway.'

'What . . . what does the bogeyman look like?' whispered Pie Face.

Snooty put on a spooky voice and said, *'He has grisly green skin and a very long nose, which drips globules of snot wherever he goes.*

He has terrible breath and rotten B.O. – when he opens his mouth, you might get KO'd!

He has hideous eyes that stare you right through, and the snot squelches out from under his shoes.'

Pie Face looked like he might cry. Jem put an arm around his shoulders.

'Don't worry,' said Snooty. 'I feel fine about it.'

The school bell rang. Snooty picked up his very expensive rucksack and walked towards the doors.

'This is the worst day ever!' said Dennis to his mates. 'First Mum tells me it's Saturday when it isn't, and then I find out one of my mates is being ghoullied! Well, I won't stand for it!'

'He's made up his mind, Dennis,' said Jem. 'We have to help him do what he wants now.'

'No way!' said Dennis. 'Beanotown is where Snooty belongs and he's not leaving without a fight!'

Gnuh-oh! Here we gno again!

Chapter Two

THE KIDS ARE ALL FRIGHT!

By the time school was
over, the Gazette's story
seemed to have spread all
round the country.

Ghost hunters and
spook seekers were pouring
into Beanotown by bus,
train and even helicopter!

'We can have some fun
with these people!' said
Dennis. 'Come on, let's raid

the drama department's costume room!'

Five minutes later, the gang were on the streets . . . disguised as zombies!

The terrified tourists had never actually
found any ghosts or spooks before, so they
didn't know whether to take selfies with the
'zombies' or run away!

By the time they got to Gasworks Road, the pals were giggling helplessly.

'**Hee-hee!**' laughed Snooty. 'That's really cheered me up, but I have to get home now – I'm going to the city to look at a flat with my Aunt.'

Dennis, Minnie, Jem and Pie Face waved goodbye to Snooty, then their giggles turned to groans when they saw who was waiting for them outside Dennis's house – it was Walter Brown, Dennis's worst enemy.

Walter's dad is the mayor of Beanotown, which means Walter thinks he can order everyone around. Normally he would only sneer at people like Dennis, but today he was positively beaming.

'Uh-oh!' said Dennis. 'Walter looks happy. That's always bad news!'

'I have exciting news,' said Walter, completely ignoring the fact that his classmates were staggering around like zombies. 'My father the mayor—'

Dennis and his friends rolled their eyes.

'—has just agreed to buy Bunkerton Castle for an absolute song! So we Browns will no longer be living in the same street as the likes of you!'

'HOORAY!' cried Minnie.

Walter glared at her. 'As I'm practically royalty now, you must all bow in my presence.'

'No way!' said Dennis, but Minnie immediately bowed extravagantly.

Walter smirked. This was more like it.

'Just so you can get a glimpse of how the best people live, I shall give you a tour of my new castle and show you lots of things you can't afford,' he said.

And with that he turned . . . and fell flat on his face!

When Minnie had bowed before him, she had only done it so she could tie his shoelaces together! Genius!

※ ※ ※

When they got to Bunkerton Castle, the mayor was there in a hard hat, and work was already under way.

'Hello, Walter,' said Wilbur.

'Hello, Daddy,' said Walter. 'I brought my friends to show them our fabulous new home.'

'When he says "friends", does he mean us?' whispered Minnie.

'We won't be living here,' said the mayor, examining his building plans. 'I'm turning this crummy old castle into a tourist attraction and hotel! This place will be a goldmine when it opens!'

Walter was crushed. All his dreams of
moving out of Gasworks Road had been
whipped away like a fart in the wind.

'Come on,' said Wilbur haughtily. 'I'll give
you the grand tour!'

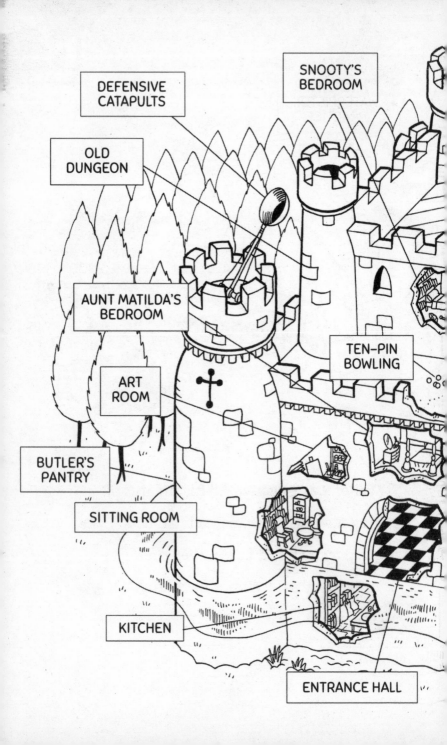

DEFENSIVE CATAPULTS

SNOOTY'S BEDROOM

OLD DUNGEON

AUNT MATILDA'S BEDROOM

TEN-PIN BOWLING

ART ROOM

BUTLER'S PANTRY

SITTING ROOM

KITCHEN

ENTRANCE HALL

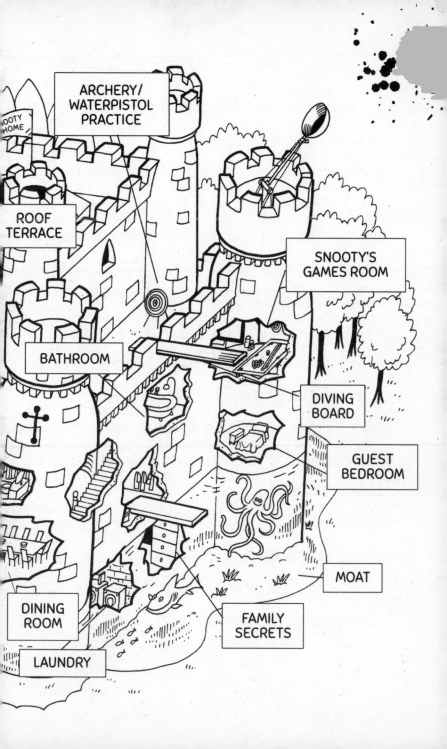

ARCHERY/
WATERPISTOL
PRACTICE

SNOOTY
HOME

ROOF
TERRACE

SNOOTY'S
GAMES ROOM

BATHROOM

DIVING
BOARD

GUEST
BEDROOM

DINING
ROOM

MOAT

FAMILY
SECRETS

LAUNDRY

Wilbur led them through his new castle, describing how he would convert the great hall into a tea room, and the drawing room into a gift shop. The room Snooty used as his personal cinema and gaming room was to become the staff toilets.

'That's a poo idea,' whispered Pie Face.

'There will be SPOOKY music playing,' said Wilbur, 'and HORRIFYING dummies lurking around every corner, waiting to scare my customers stupid – or maybe I should say scare them *even stupider*! Haw-haw!'

Dennis pointed at a limp dummy that was slumped on a chair.

'If that's one of your horrifying dummies, you won't be scaring anybody!' he said.

'You'd be better off letting Walter roam the corridors – he's *much* creepier!'

'Shut up, Dennis!' said Walter. 'When it's finished, this place will be the best haunted castle in the world. After all, you haven't seen the main attraction – the bogeyman!'

'I hope you don't change too much,' said Jem. 'It might be old, but it's been the

Bunkertons' family home for centuries.'

'That reminds me,' said Wilbur. 'I'm thinking of changing the castle's name – to *Brownkerton* Castle!'

'Oh, I love it!' Walter said, clapping his hands.

The mayor stomped off to make sure his workmen weren't taking any unauthorised breathing breaks, leaving the kids in a long corridor lit only by torches on the walls.

'This place is soooo lame!' giggled Dennis. Minnie pulled a face at a suit of armour.

And then the torches flickered and went out, plunging them into darkness.

Suddenly, a mighty, booming voice rang out:

LEAVE THIS PLACE!

The hair on the back of Dennis's neck stood on end.

'W-was that you, Minnie?' he demanded.

'No,' whispered Minnie.

'What was that?' cried Walter. Dennis turned on the torch on his phone.

'Let's get out of here!' said Jem. 'It's a bit creepy down here.'

When they'd sprinted from the castle back into the daylight, they stopped for breath.

'See?' wheezed Walter. 'If you still think this place is lame, try staying here for a night! If you can last till morning, you can stay for free. If you can't, you pay full price!'

Get the smell of luxury in your nostrils
when you stay at the beautiful

BUNKERTON CASTLE

PRICE LIST (per night)

Single Room – £500
Double Room – £1,000 (duh!)
Room with View of the Moat – £1,500
Room with View of the Goat – £800
Penthouse – £1,000,000
(a discount may be available for VIPs)

SPECIAL OFFER! Save £100 if you
clean your own toilet!

To Walter's surprise, Dennis agreed.

'We'll do it!' he said. 'On one condition.'

'Name it,' scoffed Walter.

'You have to stay the night too,' said Jem, realising the trap Dennis had set for Walter.

Walter's face went as white as a polar bear in a blizzard.

'Okay,' he said, weakly. 'Be back here at eight o'clock. I'll get Parkinson the butler to prepare us a room.'

'**WOOHOO!**' cried Dennis. 'A night in a spooky castle – just what I always *haunted!*'

Chapter Three

WHO'S AFRAID OF THE BIG BAD BOGEYMAN?

Leaving Walter at the castle, the pals rushed home to pack their overnight bags.

Dennis's mum wanted to know where he was staying, who else was going to be there and when he would be back. Once he'd told her, leaving out the bit about the terrifying bogeyman, she gave him permission to stay over at the castle.

'Permission for the most awesome spooky night in a castle ever!' said Dennis to Gnasher when they got up to his room.

Once he'd packed the essentials for a night away, he ran back downstairs and headed out to meet the rest of the Bogeyman Busters.

DENNIS'S OVERNIGHT ESSENTIALS

Gnasher - do not forget!!!
Phone + charger
Catapult
Ammo (peas, peanuts, tomatoes)
Spare ammo
Comic to read
Snacks
Doggy Snacks
Whoopee Cushion
Picture of Mum (kidding!)
P.S. Do not forget Gnasher!

Pie Face was waiting for him at the gate.

'Ready to face the bogeyman, Pie Face?' asked Dennis cheerfully.

'I'm not sure,' said Pie Face. 'I'd prefer a *pie*man to a bogeyman, every time! Although, I did notice that there was *bogeyman pie* on the menu at the tearoom, and I'd like to try that.'

He licked his lips.

BOGEY BITES TEA ROOM
BOGEY-MENU

CHILLING CHEESE ON TOAST ~ 18.00
SPINE-CHILLING SPAG BOL ~ 25.00
HAUNTED HAM SALAD ~ 19.00
BOGEYMAN PIE ~ 17.50
VILE VEGAN DISH OF THE DAY ~ 17.50
PUTRID PUDDING ~ 10.00
TERRIFYING TEA ~ 5.00
CASTLE COFFEE ~ 5.00
CREEPY COLA ~ 5.00

'I don't believe in the bogeyman,' said Minnie, skidding her scooter to a halt. 'It'll just be draughts coming in through the old windows making spooky noises, or maybe Snooty's eaten some cheese before he goes to bed or something.'

'It would be cool if he was real though,' said Dennis.

'Who says it's a man?' Minnie replied, arms crossed. 'It could be a bogeygirl, for all we know! Now, *her* I could believe in! She'd be much scarier – and better looking.'

'**PFF!** *You're* a bogeygirl,' said Dennis.

Jem came skipping down the street. She never just walked if she could do something more energetic. Jem likes to look after herself.

That's why she's so active. She likes to be fit, happy and healthy, and she thinks it's worth putting in a bit of effort.

'Do you believe in the bogeyman?' Minnie asked her.

'I'm keeping an open mind,' said Jem. 'I figure that's the healthiest outlook on this.'

JEM'S RULES 4 A HEALTHY LIFE

1. Don't lie down — sit up!
2. Don't sit — stand!
3. Don't stand — walk!
4. Don't walk — run!
5. Don't run — hop!
6. Don't hop — hop + skip!
7. Don't hop + skip — hop, skip + jump!
8. Don't hop, skip + jump — fly!
9. Er . . . when I can fly, there might be a Rule 9

'Well, what I believe is that tonight's going to be fun,' Dennis said. 'And that's good enough for me.'

Is gnobody going to ask me what I think?

They made their way back to Bunkerton Castle, stopping at Beanotown Burgers, where they ordered Slopper-Gnosher Gut-Bustin' Bean Burgers (with an extra shot of beans on top). Pie Face added an apple pie to his meal, because he likes to get his five a day.

Five pies a day, that is. He wasn't too worried about getting five fruits and vegetables.

PIE-FIVE WITH PIE FACE – GET YOUR FIVE A DAY!

BREAKFAST – BACON AND EGG PIE

LUNCH – FIVE ALIVE BLOAT PIE (BROCCOLI, LEEK, ONION, ASPARAGUS AND TOMATO PIE)

DINNER – STEAK PIE

SUPPER – APPLE PIE

MIDNIGHT SNACK – PIE PIE

Walter was waiting for them at the drawbridge, his chest puffed out proudly.

'It's the least scary castle ever, isn't it?' said Jem.

'We're going in the back door,' said Walter, leading them around the outside of the castle walls. 'Daddy had a new carpet put down in the front entrance and he doesn't want it to get dirty.'

'Crumbs!' trembled Pie Face. 'You wouldn't think this was the same castle!'

The back door was locked from the inside. Walter tugged on a thick rope that hung at the side.

The door creaked open and a dim light trickled out. A figure stood in the doorway, holding a candlestick. It cast a long and sinister shadow over the kids.

'YOU RANG?' the figure boomed.

'It's . . . it's me. Walter,' stammered Walter.

'So it is,' said the figure, sounding distinctly unimpressed. 'Oh, *goody!*'

'Well? Aren't you going to let us in?' demanded Walter.

The figure stayed silent just long enough to make Walter think that he might *not* be let in, and then stepped to one side.

'Of course, Master Walter,' said the figure, bowing ever so slightly. 'This way.'

They were IN!

Chapter Four

DON'T SPOOK UNLESS YOU'RE SPOOKEN TO!

The gloomy figure was Parkinson, Snooty's butler, who it seemed would be staying at the castle.

'I don't think he likes us,' Dennis said to Minnie as they followed him through the corridors of the castle.

'Why is he carrying a candle?' asked Minnie. 'Don't they have electricity?'

'Daddy said the electricians were doing a lot of work to the wiring,' said Walter. 'Maybe they haven't finished.'

He tried a lightswitch. **BZZZZZZT!!!**

'Nope, not finished,' he said.

'I've lit the fire in the drawing room, Master Walter,' said Parkinson.

'And put the sleeping bags down.'

'Excellent,' said Walter. 'If you could bring us some supper, that would be good. What time do you finish work in the evening?'

'Half an hour ago, sir,' said the butler, pointedly looking at his watch.

'Forget supper!' said Dennis. 'We've got some snacks with us.'

'Very good, sir,' said Parkinson. 'If only all my guests were so thoughtful.' And he looked at Walter, with one eye. It's a neat trick, if you can do it.

The castle was very dark. In the gloom, portraits of Snooty's ancestors stared down at them from the walls.

Dennis could have sworn their painted eyes followed him as he walked past. He shivered.

They made their way through the great
hall, where suits of armour were on display, all
holding real battle swords, their sharp edges
glinting menacingly in the candle light.

Jem was impressed. 'I don't know how they
could fight with those heavy suits on,' she
said. 'They must have been mega-strong!'

Just then, the knight closest to her wobbled
back and forth, then toppled from its stand.
The sword it held above its head plummeted
down towards Jem.

'Gnasher!' cried Dennis, realising he couldn't help Jem himself, but knowing that Gnasher might be able to.

Gnasher leaped towards Jem and bit the sword in two.

The two halves of the sword fell to the floor, harmlessly landing on either side of Jem.

'Clever boy!' said Dennis. Jem gave Gnasher a hug.

I don't like this, thought Gnasher. **that was too close for comfort!**

'Do be careful,' said Parkinson, as though he thought it would serve Jem right if the sword had cut her in two!

43

Parkinson opened a huge door and showed them into a grand room.

There were bookshelves filled with ancient books, sofas and reading tables. A mighty fire crackled and popped in a massive stone fireplace, casting dancing shadows around the room. An oil painting of a man in funny clothes stared down at them from above the fireplace. It was one of Snooty's ancestors.

'Is that what Snooty will look like when he's older?' asked Pie Face.

'That is the first Earl of Bunkerton,' said Parkinson. 'He died in very peculiar circumstances shortly after that portrait was painted.'

'He's *wearing* very peculiar *clothes* in the picture,' remarked Dennis. 'What a guff-head!'

'Actually,' said Parkinson. 'The Earl left a note in his diary saying he had discovered the door to a secret passageway in this very room. Being a very foolish Earl, he decided to explore.'

*The Diary of
the Earl of Bunkerton
Aged 53¾*
Ye March 25, 1745

*Exciting news – I found a
SECRET PASSAGE in the walls
of the castle! It's spooky and
smells like a toilet!*

*I shall exploreth it tomorrow!
What could possibly
go wrong?*

*P.S. Sorry about the spulling.
I was not goode at skool.*

'What did he find?' asked Minnie, eagerly.

'Unfortunately, all he found was his doom. The Earl was never seen again. It is presumed that the door to the passageway somehow closed, trapping him inside. And that was that.'

'The bogeyman!' whispered Dennis.

'What?' said Walter, who was shivering, despite the warmth of the fire.

'Don't you see?' said Dennis, his eyes sparkling. 'The Earl was never found. His tortured ghost still wanders this castle, looking for a way to escape!'

'But he can't do that!' said Walter, indignantly. 'It's my dad's castle now!'

'Rubbish!' said Minnie. 'I bet he got fed up of wearing stupid clothes and decided to run away and become a pirate or something. The note was just to put people off the scent.'

'What do you think, Parkinson?' asked Jem, turning to the old butler.

'It's possible,' he sniffed. 'The Bogeyman of Bunkerton Castle has tormented the family ever since the first Earl vanished, so his ghost is presumed to be the bogeyman.'

'Bit of a weird story,' said Dennis. 'But I say we crack open the snacks and . . .'

WOOOOOOAAAAAAHHHHH!

'What was that?' cried Pie Face.

'It was your bum!' said Minnie.

'That doesn't even make sense,' said Dennis. 'Don't worry, Pie Face, it was probably just the pipes . . .'

WOOOOOAAAAARRRRR!

'. . . Or maybe not,' finished Dennis.

Jem moved closer to the fire, wrapping her arms around herself. 'I've got a bad feeling about this,' she said. 'Is the castle always as noisy as this, Parkinson?'

But Parkinson was gone.

'Where did he go?' cried Pie Face. 'Did anyone see him leave?'

'Look,' said Dennis. 'Let's calm down. We've got candles, we've got a fire, and we've got good company – apart from Walter.'

Walter looked too scared to respond.

'Things could be a lot worse, right?' said Dennis almost convincingly.

And then . . .

FUFF!

The candles went out.

And so did the fire.

'Things just got a lot spookier,' said Minnie,
not very helpfully.

Chapter Five

THE DARK FRIGHT!

Dennis held his breath. He didn't mind a bit of excitement, but this was different. Gnasher was growling, and that usually meant something was wrong.

'What's that?' Dennis whispered, when a strange, clacking sound reached his ears.

'Your bum!' Minnie retorted, snickering.

'S-s-sorry!' Pie Face said. 'It's m-m-my teeth chattering.'

Then, as their eyes adjusted to the dim
light of the moon shining in through the
window, they suddenly became aware of
a figure standing in front of the fireplace,
looming over them.

The figure was tall, hunched and
menacing. A hood covered most of its head,

but a pair of ghoulish eyes blazed from beneath the cowl. Its lips curled in a terrible sneer, and its long nose dripped a cold, slimy substance from the tip.

'Is it the bogeyman?' said Pie Face.

'Well, it isn't the tooth fairy!' said Jem.

Gnasher growled and advanced towards the horrible sight.

'What do you want?' said Dennis.

'Get out of my castle!' the bogeyman boomed angrily.

'And what if we won't?' said Minnie. No one bosses Minnie or her friends around.

The bogeyman paused. It clearly wasn't used to being challenged.

'Just get out of my castle,' it repeated, 'and make sure the world knows that the Bogeyman

of Bunkerton Castle is back, and I'm here
to stay!'

And, with a cackle, the bogeyman
vanished. The room was dark and silent
once more.

They found some matches and lit the
candles and fire once more.

'That guy needs to work on his people
skills,' said Jem. She stooped to examine

the little puddle of slimey liquid that the
bogeyman had left behind.

'Bogeys?' asked Minnie.

'Almost definitely,' Jem confirmed.

'Cool! Bogeyman bogeys!' Minnie
exclaimed, leaning in for a closer look.

'Is it gone?' said a muffled voice that came
from somewhere near the bottom of Walter's
sleeping bag.

'It's gone,' said Dennis. 'You can come
out now.'

Walter reverse-burrowed his way out of the sleeping bag and looked around nervously.

'I hope this night doesn't have any more surprises for us,' he said.

A loud RUMBLE sent him scurrying back to the bottom of his sleeping bag.

'It's all right, Walter,' laughed Dennis. 'It's just Gnasher's tummy – he must be hungry!'

'WHOOPS!' said Pie Face. 'I might have accidentally eaten all of Gnasher's treats.'

'You ate dog treats?' asked Minnie disbelievingly. Even she wouldn't try those.

'I was nervous,' said Pie Face. 'What with the ghostly apparition and all that. They weren't bad, either.'

'Where are the kitchens, Walter?' asked Dennis, pulling his rucksack over his

shoulders. 'I'll have to get Gnasher something to eat.'

'You're going to walk around this dark castle?' asked Walter.

'When Gnasher's gotta eat, Gnasher's gotta eat!' said Dennis.

'They're in the basement,' said Walter, handing Dennis a map of the castle. The stairs are at the other end of the corridor.'

'We won't be long,' said Dennis. He lifted a candlestick and opened the door.

It was cold and dark in the corridor outside. Dennis held up his candle and consulted the old map.

'It should be along this way,' he said to Gnasher, pointing to the right.

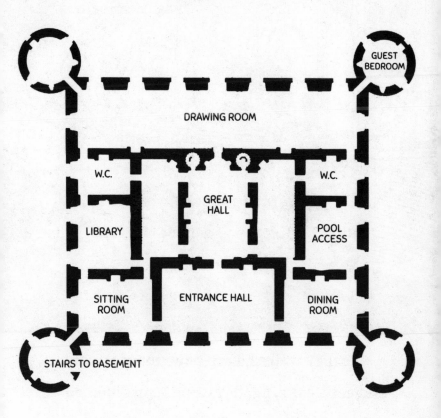

GUEST
BEDROOM

DRAWING ROOM

W.C.

W.C.

GREAT
HALL

LIBRARY

POOL
ACCESS

SITTING
ROOM

ENTRANCE HALL

DINING
ROOM

STAIRS TO BASEMENT

The candle cast a faint glow that barely
stretched far enough ahead to show Dennis
where he was putting his feet.

As they walked, each new suit of armour and eerie painting they came across loomed out of the darkness and gave them a start.

'Has this creepiness put you off your food yet, Gnasher?' Dennis asked, a little hopefully.

Gno!

After walking for what seemed like miles, they came to the stairs that led down to the kitchens. Half-way down, Dennis could hear voices. He signalled to Gnasher to be quiet and crept to the bottom of the steps. The pals peered around the corner into a room with an open door.

Inside, Parkinson and Wilbur were looking at a laptop computer.

'We're fully booked for ghost tours right into the summer,' said Wilbur.

'And 96% of the hotel rooms are booked as well,' said Parkinson.

'I knew this place was a goldmine,' said Wilbur. 'The bogeyman returning has certainly boosted sales.'

Gnasher's tummy gave a monstrous rumble. **GROWL!**

RUMBLE!

'What was that?' said Wilbur.

Dennis and Gnasher pushed themselves back into the darkness, hoping they wouldn't be discovered.

'Well, I think I'll be going home now,' said Wilbur eventually, picking up the laptop.

'Very good, sir,' said Parkinson politely. 'I'll see you out.'

When the two men had left, the pals stepped out of the gloom and into the light.

Wow, thought Dennis. *Sounds like Wilbur is actually happy his new castle is haunted.*

'That tummy of yours, Gnasher!' laughed Dennis. 'The kitchen is the next room along. Let's grab some grub and get back to the gang. I hope the bogeyman hasn't made a nuisance of himself again!'

Chapter Six

A FUNNY BUSINESS!

Dennis and Gnasher's epic journey to the kitchen was a great success. Dennis stuffed his rucksack full of goodies from the cupboards and Gnasher scoffed a plate of sausages from the fridge.

'That'll stop your tummy making any more noises,' said Dennis.

'**BOOOORRRRRP!**' burped Gnasher.

'Pity about the other parts of you!' Dennis ruffled his BFF's fur affectionately.

When they got back to the drawing room, Dennis turned his rucksack upside down and emptied the goodies onto the rug in front of the fire.

'Here we go!' he said. 'There's a pie in there somewhere for you, Pie Face. I don't know what kind it is.'

'Ooh!' said Pie Face. ' Doesn't matter what kind, I have trust in the crust!'

As they sat eating their snacks, Minnie poked Dennis in the ribs.

'Come on, cuz,' she said. 'Did you see anything out there?'

'I did, actually,' said Dennis. 'I saw the old butler dude and Wilbur. It seems like the castle's all booked up for months. The bogeyman returned just in time to make Wilbur a fortune, it seems.'

'Lucky for him!' said Jem.

'Luck has nothing to do with it,' said Walter. 'My dad has impeccable business timing. Sometimes it seems like he can see into the future, like that time he built the doughnut factory just before Mr Ring was evicted from his little doughnut shop on the high street.'

'But it was your dad who evicted him!' said Jem. 'He built the factory because he knew he was going to put poor Mr Ring out of business!'

'Business is business,' said Walter. 'If Mr Ring didn't want to be evicted, all he had to do was buy the shop. It's not my dad's fault Mr Ring didn't have the necessary one million pounds, is it?'

'RUBBISH!' said Minnie. 'Mr Ring made

great doughnuts and your dad's are rubbish. And he's so greedy, I bet he's even tried to sell the holes out of the middle!'

'Didn't you know?' said Dennis. 'Wilbur tried that, but people wouldn't pay something for nothing.'

'Just wait,' said Walter. 'My dad's doughnut-hole factory will be a winner one day!'

Jem was rummaging in her overnight bag.

'What are you looking for, Jem?' asked Pie Face.

'Rubi gave me something she said might come in handy,' said Jem, producing six pairs of goggles from the rucksack. 'They're night-vision goggles!'

She handed the goggles round. 'We're going on a ghost hunt!'

The goggles turned everything a strange green colour.

'This is great!' said Dennis. 'If that bogeyman turns up now, he won't know what's hit him!'

When they'd all stepped out into the corridor, Minnie locked the door to the drawing room.

They headed back towards the great hall,

where the sword had almost hit Jem. Just as
they opened the door, there was a mighty
CLANG! Followed by lots of smaller
metallic sounds.

CLATTER! TINKLE! CRASH!
'WAAHHHH!' shrieked the friends.

'Take it easy!' said Dennis. 'It was just
some more armour falling over.'

There was a second gap in the line of
armour where another suit had toppled over.

As they examined the collapsed suit of
armour, Minnie noticed a thread tied around
its helmet.

'This thread,' said Minnie. 'It's snapped.'

She looked up at the wall where the armour
had stood. There was a nail on the wall with
some more thread tied around it.

'And the other end is tied around that nail,'
she said. 'The armour was just too heavy for the
thread and it broke. Nothing spooky about it.'

'It's pretty scary if it's your head in the
way,' said Jem.

WOOOOAAAAHHHH!

The horrid moaning noise they'd heard
earlier rang out, echoing in the draughty old hall.

'**AAARRRGGGHH!**' yelled the friends.

Pie Face looked at one of the windows. He put his hand to it and pressed outwards.

Wind rushed through the gaps between the window and the frame, making it vibrate.

'Minnie was right,' said Pie Face 'It's just the draughty old windows.'

'These night-vision goggles are ruining everything,' said Dennis. 'At this rate, there will be nothing left to be scared of!'

Pie Face shivered. 'I'm cold,' he said. 'Let's go back to the drawing room. At least it's warm in there.'

The others agreed, so they made their way back and stood in front of the fire to get warm, relieved to take off the night goggles – they weren't very comfortable.

'Did you move my sleeping bag, Dennis?' asked Walter suddenly. 'It's not where I left it.'

'Why would I do that?' replied Dennis.

'Mine has gone too,' said Jem, pointing to where she had left it.

'They're all gone!' cried Pie Face.

Gnasher growled, looking at the farthest wall, which was cloaked in gloom. Dennis picked up a candlestick and advanced slowly towards the wall.

His eyes widened when he saw what Gnasher's sharp eyes had picked out. Their sleeping bags had been hung from the ceiling, and each had a letter painted on it. The letters spelled out a frightening message . . .

'Who did that?' squealed Pie Face.

'We locked the door,' said Minnie. 'No one could get in!'

Dennis knelt and stuck his fingers into a

little blob of green slime lying on the floor
beneath the hanging sleeping bags.

'The bogeyman,' he said grimly. 'We might
have solved the other mysteries, but the
biggest one of all is still roaming this castle!'

Chapter Seven

A STING IN THE TALE

They took down their sleeping bags. Pie Face climbed into his to see if he could stop shivering, but it didn't help.

'I'm freezing,' said Pie Face.

'Maybe we should just go home,' said Jem. 'This castle is a death-trap!'

'We could, and we'd be total failures,' said Dennis. 'Or we can make the best of it and try to have some fun. How about a ghost story?'

'Is it scarier than the one we're living through right now and don't know the ending of?' asked Minnie sarcastically.

'Definitely!' said Dennis, with relish.

'I call it . . .'

THE FEROCIOUS FIEND
OF FARTMOOR!

Once upon a time, there was a spooky old moor called Fartmoor. The moor was said to be haunted by a ferocious beast that only appeared when there was a full moon. The beast was half-man, half-wolf and half-vampire.

> Ed: Dennis's maths sometimes lets him down.

The beast's eerie cries sounded a lot like a big dog that was very, very hangry (hungry + angry = hangry). No one knew what the beast looked like, for no one who saw it ever lived to tell the tale.

People were terrified that they would be the beast's next victim. It was said it moved so silently, you never knew it it was there . . . until it was too late.

And, just before it gobbled up its latest victim, it unleashed a ghastly howl . . .

AWOOOOOOOOOOOOOOOOOOO!!!!

Jem, Minnie, Pie Face and Walter leaped almost out of their skins. Dennis rolled on the floor laughing. His faithful dog had sneaked behind his friends and supplied the bloodcurdling howl at the perfect moment!

'Gotcha!' cried Dennis, wiping his eyes. He high-fived the giggling Gnasher.

Jem patted herself on the chest. 'PHEW! You had me there, Den!' she said.

Pie Face agreed. 'Best ghost story ever! I hope I never hear it again!'

'You didn't get me,' said Minnie, although she had grabbed Walter and hidden behind him, hoping the were-hound would eat him first and leave her till later.

Walter yanked himself free and adjusted his clothes. 'Enough ghost stories,' he said. 'Let's do something else.'

'No one is going to get to sleep,' said Minnie, 'so I say we explore a bit more. If we split up, we can cover most of the castle. I'll take the top floor, because . . . because I deserve the penthouse suite.'

'I'll take the library,' Jem volunteered. 'I love old libraries.'

'I can have a look at the ground floor, I suppose?' said Pie Face doubtfully.

'We'll take the basement,' said Dennis. 'The kitchen's down there and I think Gnasher could handle a couple more sausages.'

'What about you, Walter?' asked Minnie.

'I'll take the toilet,' said Walter. 'But I'm not exploring. I'm going to lock myself in there until you all come back!'

Chapter Eight

BOOGERS, BANGERS AND BOOKS!

The long hallways of Bunkerton Castle were cold and dark, with shadows looming like creatures of the night. Even Count Dracula would have felt nervous living there!

The heavy wooden doors creaked when opened. The first room Jem peeked into was illuminated by moonlight and looked like it was infested with spooky ghosts! But it was only ancient furniture and suits of armour covered with white dust sheets and a window left open, creating a breeze.

As she gently closed the door, she was disturbed by a noise from farther along the corridor. It sounded like a ginormous rasping pump, but as she got closer to the source, it was someone noisily blowing their nose: the bogeyman!

Jem pressed herself in against the wall as much as she could and breathed a sigh of relief as he exited and headed in the opposite direction. He accidentally left a trail of loo roll unravelling, which she silently followed as the bogeyman swept around a corner.

Jem scampered to catch up and heard the loud slam of a door as she followed in his footsteps.

SLAM!

Ye Gents

© CAUTION: MEDIEVAL PLUMBING (AND LOO ROLL) INSIDE!

The loo roll ended but disappeared underneath a door, with a shiny brass sign, engraved: LIBRARY.

She tried turning the handle very slowly and extremely quietly. But she stopped herself. She was a risk taker, but not this much of a risk taker! Instead, Jem bent down and peeped in carefully through the keyhole.

She braced herself for what she expected to be a fearsome sight, only to discover the bogeyman was in fact quietly reading a very large, very old book.

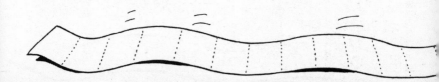

He was being careful not to allow his snot to drip onto the pages, pulling at the loo roll, square by square.

Jem watched and waited. She didn't know

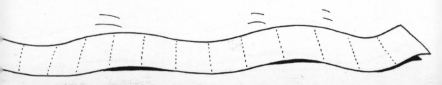

what for, but there was no way the bogeyman could escape from the library without jumping out of the third-floor windows. He was good at dripping, but that was serious dropping!

But Jem didn't pay enough attention, because she hadn't noticed she was standing on the loo roll on her side of the door! When the bogeyman next went to wipe his nose, the loo roll went tight, like a fishing line that had caught a great white shark. He walked over to the door and Jem suddenly found herself eyeball to eyeball with him, with only the door between them!

His eye locked upon her like a laser target and he threw the book he was reading directly at the door. Jem felt the entire door shudder with the force of impact and tumbled back,

tripping over her own feet, landing in a heap. She expected the bogeyman to emerge straight after, but the library seemed to have gone eerily quiet.

Jem decided to take another risk and peered back through. The bogeyman had vanished into thin air! She gasped. Then gulped. A hand was resting on her shoulder . . .

'Only me!' smiled Pie Face. 'I haven't seen a thing. I'm beginning to think we've scared the bogeyman off. I think it's time we all went back for a

pie supper. Walter says the butler will bring anything we ask for.'

Jem rolled her eyes. If they'd been searching for a pieman, there would've been no stopping Pie Face.

She explained the situation and asked Pie Face to help her push the library door open. The book the bogeyman had chucked at her was blocking it, but she felt it was an important clue and wanted to give it a full examination. When they got inside, the mystery deepened. Every window was bolted shut from the inside.

Jem and Pie Face could hardly lift the huge book, but carried it back to base as they had a feeling that it might contain a clue for them to defeat their snotty enemy.

They returned to the drawing room, excited to share their news, but when they got there, the place was already in uproar as the friends competed to share tales of their own daring encounters.

Dennis explained how he'd thought Gnasher had caught a whiff of the bogeyman, as he'd snuffled along the ground like one of those robotic vacuums. Turned out Gnasher had a scent, alright: sausages in the castle's kitchen.

'Gnasher was so focussed on the bangers, he didn't spot old "Boogers" making a cup of tea. It was only when he started chucking saucers at us, we realised.'

'Realised what?' asked Minnie.

'That it was honey and lemon he was making,' Dennis replied.

'And that's relevant how?' Minnie asked.

Dennis shrugged. 'We also discovered he smells a bit like sausages.'

Minnie told how she'd followed a loud crashing noise and discovered the bogeyman trying on a suit of armour. 'I snuck up behind him like a ginger ninja, but a mouse squeaked, and then—'

'Minnie Mouse?' laughed Walter, as if he was the first person to ever crack that gag.

Minnie paused and took a deep breath before retaliating. '—it chased me. But it was slower than Walter's dad at the school sports day parent's race!'

'My father was restricted by a three-piece suit and his best brown brogues,' sniffed Walter. 'Anyway, what pathetic seekers you were – I had him trapped in a headlock, but couldn't carry him back all by myself.'

'Sure, Walter, I believe you, but millions

wouldn't,' said Pie Face.

'Walter, we all know you never take risks like that. You'd throw your granny out of a hot air balloon if you suspected it had bad altitude,' mocked Minnie.

'Throwing your gran out of a hot air balloon is the definition of bad attitude,' added Dennis.

Minnie giggled. 'I said 'altitude', not 'attitude', Dennis! It's a fancy word, meaning height.'

'Hang on,' Minnie said, suspicious now. 'We've all been in different parts of the castle, and it's BIG . . . a bogeyman can't move *that*

much quicker than us. How can he have been in so many places at roughly the same time?'

'Uh? Do you think there's maybe more than one?' asked Jem.

'Maybe there's thousands?' asked Pie Face, horror dawning on his face.

'Bunkerton Castle is infested with bogeys!" chimed Walter, sounding oddly excited.

Jem started to read out a page from the book that had been thrown at her. 'It says here that, in the olden days, the legend of the bogeyman was something grown-ups invented to scare children into being good . . .'

Dennis was shocked! 'The audacity! Tricking kids is the lowest of the low . . .'

'If Bogeymen really are fake news, you'd hope grown-ups could create a scarier imaginary monster? A bogeyman's just a pound-shop zombie,' giggled Jem. She turned back to her book again.

'Which creature would you least like to be stuck in a castle with?' Pie Face asked Minnie.

'Mrs Creecher if Gnasher has eaten your homework!' she laughed, thinking of their strict headteacher at Bash Street School.

'But what *really* makes the scariest monster?' asked Jem. 'Is it the loudness of its growl? The spikiness of its tail? The sharpness of its fangs?'

'That's enough about Gnasher, we're trying to suss out the bogeyman!' laughed Dennis.

Gnasher wagged his tail and gnashed a small gniggle.

Jem started to leaf through the history book again. Dennis spotted as her face lit up with discovery. She loudly shushed the room.

'Listen up! It says here that the Bogeyman of Bunkerton Castle is . . .'

'Standing directly behind you, you silly fools.'

The rasping voice boomed out across the room and the kids turned as one to face their foe.

The bogeyman was leaning casually against the fireplace, staring at them. Minnie gulped. He looked far scarier than Mrs Creecher . . .

Chapter Nine

BOGEY WONDERLAND!

The bogeyman snarled at the kids, 'This is your final warning.'

Traditionally, the promise of a 'final' warning only encouraged Dennis to make the most of it, cramming in as much mischief as was humanly possible before the game was up.

So he stood defiantly, arms folded. This meant he couldn't disguise the yawn that was building in his throat. Big mistake. The bogeyman seemed to inflate with rage!

'Am I boring you? You imbeciles are intruding in MY HOME.'

'Excuse me, sir,' asked Pie Face, waving a snotty tissue in the air, like a white flag of peace on a battlefield. 'What *exactly* is a limbo-seal?'

'YOU ARE!' raged the bogeyman. 'And so is your teacher, for not teaching it to you!'

Jem helpfully whispered to Pie Face, 'It's a grown-up word for a fool.'

'Phew, I thought it was something rude,' replied Pie Face.

He spotted the bogeyman was still glaring at him. He made the gesture of quickly zipping his mouth shut.

'Leave this place now, OR ELSE!' the bogeyman screeched.

'I could collect the cash from our bet if that happens,' Walter volunteered. He turned to the other kids. 'It's £100 each for the new kids annual ticket to The Haunted Mansion. Pets require their own tickets.'

The other kids knew that the price the bogeyman was talking about couldn't be paid with cash. It would be their final act if they disobeyed its orders.

'Leave now, forever! Tell the world I'm back . . . and this time it's forever!'

The bogeyman's nose started twitching. He was trying to suppress an unstoppable sneeze!

AAAAATIIISHOOOOO!

The candles flickered wildly and the room darkened briefly as the kids ducked to avoid the gross spray from his nostrils.

In the confusion, he lunged forward and ripped the book from Jem's hands.

'Hey! Snot fair! He's robbed the book!'

As her mates rushed to help, they realised the bogeyman had made a clean getaway. Well, a snotty one, but he was GONE.

Some pages torn from the book fluttered into the fireplace like vampire bats, glowing brightly, before vanishing forever . . .

'"I'm back forever, kids", BUT next sec, he's vamoosed?' said Minnie. 'I for one think he's fibbing.'

Walter disagreed. 'He warned us to to leave right now, or else! Whatever the bogeyman is, he's most definitely a grown-up, so I think we'd best do as we've been told.'

Dennis was having none of that plan. 'There are four of us . . . five, if you agree to help, Walter. I fancy our chances to bag ourselves a bogeyman. It would be rude not to

get to know him better.'

Gnasher barked for attention. 'Of course,
Gnasher you too – there are six of us. In the
olden days, stories never included the dog as
part of the team's name.'

Pie Face was inspired!
'A group of six pals who
take on dangerous missions.
The Supreme Six!'

Jem laughed and said, 'Think of this as the most exciting game of hide and seek we've ever played.'

'It'll be a game of hide and *shriek* if any of you lot find him,' mocked Walter.

Dennis thought about the flying saucers he'd faced in the kitchens. This bogeyman was as dangerous as any alien. They needed to be careful.

He told everyone, 'If big bogey butt turns nasty, head straight back here.'

Pie Face was still buzzing about his Supreme Six idea. 'We need a top-secret code word we can yell. If you hear it, we all rush

100

back here and try to take the bogeyman on as a team.'

'What's the code word?' asked Rubi.

'I know the perfect code word for this particular mission,' suggested Minnie. '**BOGEYS!** As loud as you can!'

The gang chanted as one.

'How immature,' complained Walter. 'I won't shout that.'

By the time Walter had finished rolling his eyes, the room was deserted. Apart from Pie Face, who reached out and said, 'C'mon Walter, it's time to hunt boogers!'

Jem had led Dennis and Gnasher to the library, back to the exact spot she'd earlier spotted the bogeyman.

On the way there, she told Dennis about the theory she had after reading the book that had been thrown at her earlier. It was said the Bogeyman of Bunkerton Castle had been notorious for robbing rich nobles who had visited previous generations of Snooty's family.

Terrified townspeople refused to bring supplies up to Bunkerton anymore and the soldiers who defended the castle had started to walk out.

The Duke at the time was concerned, so he decided to investigate. He discovered the castle contained a maze of secret passageways that the bogeyman had been using to creep around unseen.

The Duke soon detected the entrance and sealed it with tar, then cement. For weeks after, the castle had echoed with cries, sniffles and sneezes . . . but no one had ever been robbed again.

'**WOAH**! The bogeyman was picked, rolled and flicked!' Dennis loved history with a dash of gruesome grossness. 'But if you knew all that already, why didn't you say earlier, and why are we in here looking for the book?'

Jem huddled close to Dennis, checked carefully around, then whispered into his ear.

'We're not looking for the book,' she whispered. 'I don't know for sure, but I think he tore out the pages on the bogeyman and threw them in the fire, not realising that I'd already read them. I think he used the book as research and he didn't want us to figure him out.'

'So what are you saying?'

'I'm saying there's something very fishy about this bogeyman. What kind of bogeyman drinks tea?'

'A thirsty kind?' Dennis joked loudly.

'Shh! We don't want him to come looking for us.'

'Sorry,' Dennis whispered. 'So why are we in here?'

'He got out of here somehow before. There has to be an entrance to the secret passageways in here. Help me look for something out of place.'

They split up to search.

'Psst. Over here.' Dennis pointed up. There were thousands of books, all perfectly arranged. Their old buddy, Biggy* – the Yeti at Beanotown library – would have been wowed!

But, as Jem had suspected, there was one large gap, where the book the bogeyman had pinched clearly used to rest.

'Great job, Dennis!' She stretched up, but it was way too high for her to reach. If only Biggy

*Ed Note: Read all about Biggy in I.P. Daley's thriller in the chiller, *The Abominable Snowmenace*.

had been there right then.

She tried balancing on Dennis's shoulders, but the gap was still just out of reach. However, inside, hidden between the books, she now spied a tiny golden switch, sparkling in the moonlight. If only she could reach it.

Jem had a brainwave. 'Psst! Gnasher . . . I think someone has used a sausage as a bookmark up—'

Gnasher had zoomed up the human ladder faster than Billy Whizz, careering straight into the gap, hitting the switch with his wet black nose, before he even realised he'd been tricked.

Then the most incredible thing happened. The bookcase opened like a door with a creepy creak. Dennis rushed towards the secret passageway in excitement, totally forgetting that Jem was on his shoulders. The two tumbled to the ground in a heap. *OOOF!*

✳ ✳ ✳

Pie Face had enjoyed better sleepovers. Following Walter's lead was a risky business.

Despite his claims to have wrestled the bogeyman earlier, he was now creeping so slowly and nervously that Pie Face kept bumping into him. Walter promised the next time it happened, he was going to banish him back to the drawing room.

That suited Pie Face. He didn't enjoy exploring creepy castles and he absolutely hated the cobwebs he could see hanging from the chandeliers. He kept looking up nervously in case any ninja spiders were waiting to abseil onto his head . . .

This time the fault was equally split. Pie Face hadn't noticed Walter had suddenly paused at the top of the castle's grand marble staircase. They collided, then tumbled, tangled together like a giant ball of wool.

'I wish this was a bouncy castle,' muttered Pie Face when they came to a stop at a mid-way point on the stairs.

'Get off me, you oaf!' wailed Walter. He pushed at Pie Face, sending the two of them rolling . . .

'OOOPS!'

He'd

'YOW!'

only

'OW!'

gone

'URGH!'

and

'EEK!'

done

'ARGH!'

it

'OUCH!'

again.

As they fell, Pie Face's runny nose dripped. A dribble of stringy green snot landed on Walter's cheek. He forgot his earlier rule and screamed out in sheer disgust.

Walter had just accidentally wailed the emergency codeword signalling for the entire Supreme Six to rush back to base!

When Jem followed Dennis into the secret passage, everything suddenly became clearer to her.

Above them, shafts of faint flickering light shone in. It didn't take them long to suss out the source. There were tiny peepholes cut in the eyes of the posh portraits in the hallway. Whoever was in here could secretly watch and listen!

That was how the bogeyman knew how to always stay one step ahead. It could spy on their every move!

By standing on a box, they could just see through the eyeholes and work out how to get back to the drawing room. That way they could discover how the bogeyman was sneaking in!

All they really had to do was follow Gnasher – he was following the scent of the sausages he'd snaffled from the kitchen back to base.

They soon recognised they were alongside the main wall of the drawing room and saw a golden lever. Before Jem pulled it, Dennis told her his master plan. She was shocked.

'You want us to keep this secret from the rest of the gang? You've got to be kidding.'

'I never kid about anything,' Dennis replied, deadly serious.

Jem couldn't stop laughing as they pulled the lever. They emerged back into the drawing room alone through the fireplace.

'OK, Mr Mature – we'll do it your way . . .'

They were interrupted by an ear-shattering yell that sent shivers up their spines.

The scream was Walter. That meant Pie Face was in danger!

Dennis, Jem and Gnasher rushed towards the yell, but Minnie had already untangled Pie Face from Walter. The gang was reunited. Sort of.

'I'm sorry Walter, it was all my fault for not looking where I was going,' explained Pie Face.

'If it wasn't for you, we'd be busy tickling the bogeyman's toes to make him talk by now!' moaned Walter. 'But he's vanished . . . like a sneeze into a hanky! Something you could take a few lessons from, Pie Face.'

Dennis and Jem spoke together to everyone. 'We need to all swear an oath together.'

'I'm not allowed to swear,' said Pie Face. 'And I'm not going to start, just because I'm away at a sleepover.'

Jem explained that swearing an oath was just making a promise amongst friends. Dennis started to speak louder.

'I think the best thing we can do tonight is snuggle up . . .'

'Ewwww!' blurted out Walter.

'...and NEVER EVER TALK ABOUT WHAT WE'VE SEEN HERE AT BUNKERTON CASTLE TONIGHT.'

'What?' demanded Minnie. 'No one sleeps at a sleepover. That's the rule!'

'Since when have you ever stuck to the rules, Min?!' asked Jem.

Within seconds of getting into her sleeping bag, however, Minnie was snoring, making

a noise like a lawnmower being used to cut barbed wire!

'But this isn't what the bogeyman told us to do,' spluttered Walter in the darkness. The gang ignored his complaint as they unrolled the rest of their sleeping bags.

'Tuck in, old pal,' said Dennis to Gnasher.

Gnesh! thought Gnasher as he slobbered at the prospect of devouring the chain of twenty sausages that he'd snaffled from the kitchens earlier.

Dennis could guess his oldest pal's thoughts and chuckled. 'I meant tuck in beside me, Gnasher! I've got a plan for the sausages. We're going to spring the ultimate surprise and finish this off on a high . . ."

Dennis cosied into Gnasher. It was cold. A chilly draught was making the candles flicker. If he hadn't been so tired, he might have realised his plan was already working!

Chapter Ten

WE DON'T TALK
ABOUT BOGEYMEN

Jem rubbed her eyes drowsily. She'd awakened,
but it definitely wasn't morning time. There
were no birds singing and it was still dark.
In her imagination she could hear the urgent
flutter of vampire bats. She realised she was
shivering. It was freezing cold.

She glanced at the large grandfather clock in the corner of the drawing room. It was two o'clock in the morning.

Beside the fire, which was long extinguished, Gnasher's teeth were chattering in his sleep, clinking chaotically like a badly tuned piano.

There was a creepy mist in front of her nose. Jem realised it was in fact only her own breath condensing in the freezing temperatures.

She scanned the room and spotted her pals. Tucked up snug in their sleeping bags, they looked like a collection of steaming teapots, as their own breath fogged in the cool night air.

Nothing scared Jem. Not evil zombie veg, sinister slime monsters or terrifying robotic teachers! The truth was out there in Beanotown.

Every one of those monsters had one thing in common: Mayor Wilbur Brown was typically lurking in the background, usually as part of a sinister scheme to grab more power or money – most likely both!

Owning Bunkerton Castle definitely gave him the illusion of power – Jem suspected it wouldn't be long before he was calling himself Duke Wilbur Brown on his latest set of mayoral election posters and the cash was sure to follow if tourists believed they might lay eyes on the fabled bogeyman!

Jem shivered. More fearful fog had appeared from above and was starting to cloud her vision. She gasped fearfully as something dripped onto her head. She reached up and felt it.

'PHEW!' It was just a leak from the ancient roof. Nothing to be afraid of.

She lowered her hand to dry it and that was when she realised she was wrong. Horridly wrong!

It wasn't water on her fingers or head, but thick, green, slimy snot!

Jem quickly realised exactly who, and what, was dripping onto her.

The snivelling, snotty Bogeyman of
Bunkerton Castle!

Jem tried to remain defiant as the bogeyman bent down towards her face. She wanted to stare him out. He whispered into her ear. His breath stank of stale coffee.

'This is your last chance. Ignore your silly oath and promise to instead tell I.P. Daley the terrifying truth about me. Let her fill the Beanotown Gazette with my legend tomorrow, so people all over the world learn of me. Or let her one day write a book about the terrible revenge I took upon five nosey school children and their mangy mutt! It's your choice.'

Jem nodded weakly, as the bogeyman raised himself back to his full height. Another drop of snot was dangling from his nose, and she closed her eyes as it started to drip and stretch towards her.

The bogeyman laughed meanly.

MWAH-HA-HA!

It was the evil laughter that raised the alarm. Jem's mates instantly saw they had creepy company.

Dennis sprung his masterplan into action. 'Now, Gnasher! Get him!'

Gnasher leapt at the bogeyman, swirling sausages around him like a lasso.

With a huge gust, the candles flickered wildly and the room plunged into darkness. By the time they'd regained their full illumination, the bogeyman had disappeared.

But so had Gnasher . . .

The friends gasped as one! Even Walter seemed slightly upset . . .

'Your greedy mutt has stolen the sausages!' Walter whined.

'Trust me, he'll be back before breakfast,' replied Dennis, confidently.

Before anyone could react, they were distracted by a loud knock at the drawing room's massive wooden doors. It was an exceedingly loud thump, made by a mallet-sized fist.

Dennis puffed out his chest, strode over and flung the doors open. It was the second repulsive vision in less than five minutes, a fearsome sight none of them would soon forget.

It was Parkinson, the butler, wearing a fluffy onesie covered with a design consisting

of a pattern of pineapples with funny faces!

Parkinson dropped into a low, awkward bow, and Dennis noticed with embarrassment that his pompous wig was at risk of falling off, revealing a surprising amount of hair underneath. It now sat askew on his head.

Since when did Parkinson bow? It struck Dennis as odd that Snooty would make his butler do such a thing – he'd always described the fellow as more like a brother than staff.

'I heard shouting. I'd have thought you children would have tired yourselves out by now. Please keep the racket down. Some of us need our beauty sleep.'

Dennis stifled a laugh.

'The bogeyman was in here again,' Walter complained.

Parkinson rolled his eyes. 'I'm sure even the bogeyman requires sleep.'

'There's no way we can get back to sleep now,' said Dennis, resisting the urge to straighten Parkinson's wig – or knock it off entirely. 'But we'd love it if you'd help us rustle up a midnight feast from the kitchens! Gnasher's going to be back here in a minute, and I predict a riot if we don't have one waiting.'

Walter sulked, 'It's too late for a midnight feast. It's the middle of the night. I would rather we all just settled down and . . .'

Minnie clamped her hand over Walter's mouth and helpfully finished his sentence, '. . . tucked into a slap-up feed!'

The gang cheered as one: 'RESULT!'

But before Pie Face could even

think which pie-filling he most wanted, there was a noisy kerfuffle behind the entrance to the secret passage. As it got louder, they all recognised a sound that convinced them everything was going to turn out fine.

The halls were alive . . . with the sound of Gnasher!

GNASH! GNASH! GNASH! GNASHETY!

The bogeyman burst back into the drawing room, entangled in a string of sausages and pursued by Gnasher, who leapt to grab the last sausage in the chain between his teeth, pulling it tight around the middle of their foe, making him stumble and trip.

Dennis and Jem high-fived each other! Plan D&G had worked. They'd managed to capture the bogeyman!

The bogeyman wriggled and squirmed, but there was no escape from the string of sausages. These were Butch Butcher's Slumberland specials; so big, you need a nap after eating one. They were strong enough to tie a cruise ship up at port!

The creature realised its struggles were in vain. But it had one final trick!

It turned to Parkinson and spoke. 'Release me immediately, or I tell them everything!'

Chapter Eleven

PESKY KIDS

Jem marched directly towards the bogeyman, reached out, grabbed his nose and twisted hard! He didn't move a muscle or mutter the slightest complaint. What she did next shocked her friends even more!

She grabbed the bogeyman's scalp and pulled with all her strength. His entire head popped off, making a sound like weak fart.

Pie Face shrieked!

'Stop, Jem, please. The Headless Bogeyman of Bunkerton Castle is even more terrifying.'

Jem shook her head then smiled triumphantly. Tied up with a string of sausages, being guarded by Gnasher, was none other than Parkinson! Jem hadn't pulled off his head, but a cunning bogeyman disguise!

The true villain was unmasked!

EH?

'Huh? TWO Parkinsons!?' said Pie Face
as he looked back and forth between the two
identical grown-ups now occupying the
drawing room.

'It's Parkinson's evil twin – a bogeybutler!'
yelled Minnie.

Dennis felt his nose twitch and his menace-sense tingle. Either that, or he was about to sneeze.

Something wasn't right. Snooty had never mentioned Parkinson as having any family? The original Parkinson standing before Dennis wearing a pineapple onesie hadn't said a word. Surely he'd either try to help his twin or even admit how disappointed he was to see him trying to scare the coolest kids in town?

Dennis looked Parkinson slowly up and down, trying to get to the bottom of this mystery.

And it was Parkinson's bottom that blurted out the truth!

No, not his bum, cheeky! The things at the very *bottom* of his body . . . his feet!

The onesie-wearing Parkinson had on shiny brown shoes. The posh type reserved for teachers and businessmen. Rubbish for football, but great for stomping around with heavy self-importance. Shoes like this cost more than a year's pocket money!

Now, Dennis knew Parkinson prided himself on his appearance, and so posh shoes were to be expected . . . but surely he'd never wear them with a onesie!

What's more, Dennis spotted a familiar pattern upon them, etched into the leather. A little mountain range made by rows of

perfectly placed 'W's . . .

Dennis stared at the polished leather footwear so intently he could see the little smile forming upon his face reflected in them. He'd sussed it! This was the final clue he needed to confirm what he and Jem had already suspected.

Dennis kept his cool and calmly said, 'Parkinson, that will be all for this evening. Your "twin" can look after things here for now . . .'

Parkinson stooped into another weird, exaggerated bow, his wig slipping again to reveal thick brown hair that Dennis was now sure didn't belong to the old butler. He grabbed the wig and yanked!

Parkinson's head flew off with the wig . . . it was another mask! And beneath? Mayor Wilbur Brown!

'I can't believe it's not butler!' squealed a shocked Pie Face

Before the mayor could react, Minnie

scuttled over to tie his shoelaces together.
Like father like son, he tripped as he lunged to
grab Dennis and was left as a crumpled heap.
The indignity!

'OOPS! What a night-mayor for
Beanotown's big boss man,' sniggered Jem.

Walter rushed to help his father. 'Call
Pest Control right away, Father! This castle is
infested with disgusting creatures!' he smirked.

Jem said, 'Not anymore, Walter – we've just caught 'em!'

'He's talking about you kids. You're the disgusting creatures in this room', snarled Wilbur.

GNAAAAAAASH!

Gnasher let out a deep rumbling growl for ten full seconds!

> Try to growl for ten seconds – especially if you're reading this in public! Measure how loud it is with the Gnashometer at Beano.com

'Don't worry, Gnash, he means you too!' said Dennis, patting his mate for reassurance, missing the point – spectacularly – as always.

Jem rounded on Walter. 'You double-crosser! You knew the truth all along, didn't you?'

Walter gave a snort of contempt and a fake

cry of fear, before going to cuddle his dad, who pushed him meanly away.

The squabble was interrupted by Pie Face, who, inspired by Jem and Dennis's bravery, leapt like a monkey onto Parkinson's back before jamming his fingers deep into his nostrils. He made a sound as if he was trying force a poo whilst constipated as he attempted to unwrap what he believed was yet another cunning mask!

MMMOOOOOOHURGH!

Jem had to tickle Pie Face underneath his armpit just to make him let go! 'Stop, this isn't pass-the-parcel, that's his real face!'

'About time too,' said Pie Face.

Parkinson's eyes began to water. He was doubtful whether his nostrils would ever return to their original size after Pie Face's antics, but it was a feeling of shame that had triggered the tears. 'The game's up,' he said. 'It's time to clear things up, like the Bunkerton butler always does.'

Wilbur angrily butted in. 'Don't you dare, you silly old fool! You'll be locked up forever!'

Walter nodded and added, 'No one disobeys my father. He controls the Force . . .'

'The force?' squeaked Pie Face worriedly. He'd recently watched a movie where a bad guy used something called the force to do naughty stuff in space.

'The Beanotown Police Force, duh!' confirmed Walter proudly.

But Parkinson had had enough. 'You kids deserve an explanation. Lord Snooty deserves one more than anyone. I've let him down – I've let you all down . . .' he said miserably.

In the background a faint sizzling sound signalled things were beginning to heat up. Gnasher hadn't wasted a moment and had unravelled the sausages as soon as Parkinson promised to talk.

Dennis smiled and said to his friends, 'Well done, gang. We've discovered Bunkerton Castle's silliest sausages.' He turned around and winked at Wilbur. 'Guess this is a *wurst* case scenario for a corrupt town mayor such as yourself. After a *string* of dodgy deals, you're in deep *schnitzel*.'

'And I would have gotten away with it too, if it weren't for you pesky brats,' growled Wilbur, shaking his head in disgust.

Chapter Twelve

SNOOT DAWG

Everyone sat in the drawing room's comfy armchairs. Walter and Wilbur were far from comfortable, however, wedged as they were on one tiny armchair, with their shoelaces tied together to prevent a final sneaky getaway.

As the group munched upon their sausages, Parkinson spoke. It was a story of sadness . . . and badness.

He explained how he'd faithfully looked after Marmaduke Snooty as if he were his own son, ever since his parents, the Duke and

Duchess, mysteriously disappeared following the Great Beanotown Bank Crash.

Parkinson revealed how he'd secretly been planning to resign as the Bunkerton family butler to move to Denmark with his fiancé and fulfil his ambition of becoming a baker. But he couldn't leave young Marmaduke to fend for himself or, worse, be sent to stay with his mean Aunt Matilda unprotected. He chose Snooty.

And Parkinson's true love left for Denmark alone, never to return.

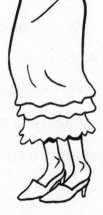

He never regretted it though – he loved Snooty as if he was his own son.

But recently, Parkinson had realised that the boy was miserable and, worst of all, lonely. The castle was isolating him from living his life.

'It's no place for a young person,' he admitted. 'The Wi-Fi speed is awful, it's cold, no one ever comes to visit . . .'

'To be fair, Parkinson,' added Minnie, 'every time we called around, you wound up the drawbridge and threatened to go medieval and throw tar over us if we came any closer.'

Parkinson explained, 'That was only because the castle was so dangerous; I could barely keep Marmaduke safe, let alone a bunch of other kids. We just didn't have the money to modernise and make the castle safe for visitors.'

'Yeah, and Snoot Doggy Dawg could never join our group chats 'cos the Wi-Fi was so rubbish!' added Dennis. 'He said you didn't want to fork out for superfast . . .'

'Snoot Doggy *what*?!' spluttered a bewildered Parkinson.

'It's what Snooty called himself online,'

revealed Dennis. 'He loved Bunkerton, but I guess he just wanted to be able to do more kids stuff. Maybe a holiday. He always says how he'd like to see more of the world – a bit like you and your girlfriend all those years ago.'

'Tom was my boyfriend. Not that it makes any difference,' replied Parkinson sadly. 'But you're right. I want those things for him too. That's why I wanted Marmaduke to leave Bunkerton and make the most of his life. He just needed a gentle push.'

Parkinson explained that he'd needed a buyer with enough money to fix the place up, so Wilbur had been the only obvious choice as he was the richest person in Beanotown. He was also the sneakiest person.

It was Wilbur who first hatched the scheme to bring back the Bogeyman of Bunkerton Castle to scare Snooty away. But Parkinson admitted he'd been a willing accomplice.

Parkinson revealed how Wilbur had found the spooky book in the library while Snooty was at school, though of course he didn't actually bother reading it, and just started asking questions instead. About the family history. About the castle. Were there any legends? Anything . . . spooky in the past?'

He told how Wilbur wanted to rewrite the

history of Bunkerton Castle to claim that a
fearsome minotaur – a half human, half cow
monster – roamed the corridors.

Wilbur interrupted, 'A minotaur burger
in the café would be far more popular than a
bogey burger! Cuddly little mini-taurs to take
home for the family. The money opportunities
were endless!'

'In the end, a bogeyman mask was the
easiest option,' Parkinson continued, ignoring

Wilbur, 'and after I tried it on and accidentally scared young Marmaduke, it soon became my only one. He announced he was leaving, and Wilbur got the castle for a bargain price the very next morning.'

Wilbur had done a deal that if Snooty was spooked enough to leave and the sale went through as planned, Parkinson would continue as the Bunkerton Butler – this was his home after all. Wilbur had loved the idea – what could show he was a genuine VIP more than his own private butler?

That way, the castle would be fixed up, Snooty would be given a fresh start, and Parkinson would have a new family to serve. It was a win, win, win!

Or so he had thought.

What he hadn't expected was Wilbur's plan to turn the castle into a spooky theme park with him being made to dress up as a bogeyman all day every day.

When Parkinson asked about what wages he could expect for all this effort, Wilbur had replied smugly, 'Wages? As if! You signed a contract stating you'd work here for free for life. Always read the small print. A deal's a deal.'

Parkinson had realised he'd been tricked and had been miserable ever since. He missed Snooty, not to mention the costume was seriously uncomfortable.

'Yeah, about the gross slime?' asked Jem. 'I take it that was just fake snot from Har Har's

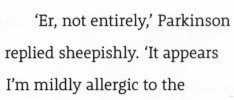

joke shop?'

'Er, not entirely,' Parkinson replied sheepishly. 'It appears I'm mildly allergic to the

mask, and it made my nose run like
a waterfall!'

Jem looked 100% grossed-out.
'Ewwwwwwww! I want a bath!'

Her friends chuckled, until they were
interrupted by a large rumble coming from the
ceiling above.

Gnasher barked noisily, as if he was trying
to warn them of something dangerous.

'What's that?' said Jem.

'The castle's falling down – it's cursed,'
cried Walter.

Parkinson interrupted and motioned for
calm. 'The drawbridge is up and I have the
only key.' He pulled out a massive key he was
wearing like a medallion from underneath
his bogeyman costume.

That's when the footsteps started approaching from the secret passageway.

TIP TAP. TIP TAP.

But everyone was together inside the drawing room now, so it could mean only one thing . . . surely it couldn't be the *real* bogeyman?

Wilbur and Parkinson's teeth chattered, but it wasn't cold anymore . . .

Chapter Thirteen

TALE OF WOAH

The footsteps grew ever louder. The real
bogeyman was getting ever closer.

Pie Face tried to swing the fireplace shut, but it was an impossible task. He yelled for Dennis, Minnie and Jem to help, but it wouldn't budge.

Whatever it was that was coming for them, was now unstoppable.

Wilbur and Walter were hiding behind the large leather armchair in the corner of the room, cowering.

Parkinson stood bravely and motioned Jem, Minnie, Dennis and Pie Face to get behind him. He picked up a heavy iron poker from beside the fire and stood like a baseball player preparing to hit a home run.

A huge sneeze from the approaching
monster made them all nearly jump out of
their skin! Any second now, they'd face the
fearsome creature . . .

A short, skinny figure emerged into the half-light, its brown furry head ducking through the fireplace entrance. They all held their breath. Was it a werewolf? Were bogeymen actually furry? Only, it wasn't fur at all . . . It was hair.

'That's certainly not cricket, old chap.'

Parkinson dropped the poker mid-swing and smiled with delight! It was Marmaduke, Lord Snooty, the former Earl of Bunkerton Castle!

Dennis beamed triumphantly and held up his phone, displaying the Whassup! Messenger app for everyone to witness.

He'd sent Snooty an urgent DM (Dennis-Message) telling him his old pal Parkinson was in a pickle. Snooty had headed back to Beanotown immediately by helicopter.

'I landed on the battlements directly above. Bananaman guided me in through the spooky mist outside,' he explained as he high-fived Dennis, Jem, Minnie, Pie Face and Gnasher.

That explained the terrifying bump in the night.

'I'm back for good. The only legends at Bunkerton will be you and I, Parkinson. The best family in the world!'

It was at this point that Parkinson demonstrated you can't take the 'but' away from the butler.

He reminded, 'But you don't own Bunkerton anymore, Marmaduke . . . You'll have to pay to get in and be scared like everyone else nowadays.'

The friends glared at Wilbur. Minnie spoke first, 'Mayor Brown, you have the power to fix this.'

Wilbur looked up and grinned. 'OK, now you put it like that. I'll sell it straight back . . .'

Snooty couldn't believe his luck! But before he could reply, Wilbur quickly added, 'AS IF!'

Walter sneered and took centre stage in the negotiations. 'It'll cost you double what father paid,' he said smugly. His smarminess evaporated when Wilbur shoved him aside and changed the deal.

'We want ten times what we paid. Our builders have nearly finished the upgrade, and the castle now has the fastest Wi-Fi in town.'

'DONE!' said Snooty, sticking his hand out to shake on the deal.

'Here, sign this agreement I've drawn up on my phone. You're right, the Wi-Fi is fast,' said Jem, thrusting a phone out at Wilbur, who took it greedily and quickly scrawled his signature on the screen. Snooty calmly signed it too.

'DEAL!' Wilbur smirked.

Snooty smirked straight back at him.

Wilbur started to feel he'd maybe made a grave mistake. How much had his repairs actually cost him? But it was too late. Snooty smirked, smiled, grinned and then chuckled. He was delighted!

'Thank you for your extreme generosity, Mayor Brown.'

'What?!'

'I can cover the fee easily from the money I made selling my unwanted family art in

London. Two paintings of Aunt Matilda sold for over ten million pounds! The walls of the National Portrait Gallery have never looked more judgemental.'

Parkinson was stunned. He knew Marmaduke couldn't stand those spooky old paintings – he'd been storing them out of sight in the attic for years – but he didn't think Snooty would ever sell them.

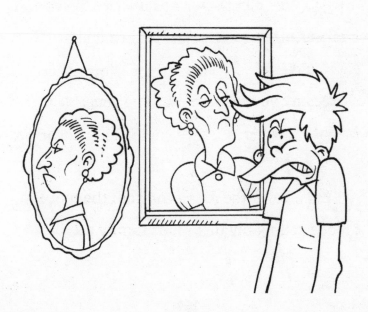

But what Snooty revealed next really made everything seem worthwhile.

'Most importantly,' added Snooty, 'Thanks to your efforts in convincing everyone that the castle is haunted, Bunkerton has just been voted the World's Best Spooky Destination!'

A weird look appeared on Wilbur's face as Snooty continued to troll him. He looked as if he'd just pooped his pants.

'On the way back in the helicopter, I even planned our merch. Thanks to the Whizz-speed Wi-Fi, I was able to upload it while we've been talking, and they're already selling like hot dogs.'

'You mean, selling like hot cakes?' checked Jem.

'No. Like hot dogs. Gnasher's Monster Dogs – based on the sausages Dennis told me he used to capture a monster. Soon to be on sale in the Terrifying Tea Room and Ghoulish Gift Shop! Result!'

'Oh, and Dennis has messaged the famous writer, I.P. Daley. She wants to write a horror novel for kids, inspired by everything that's happened here.'

'A book about the villainy of the Bunkerton

Bogeymonster that I, Wilbur Brown, created?
How magnificent. I'm a creative genius!' The
mayor punched the air in triumph. Even when
he was a loser, he always attempted to find
some pathetic way to claim victory.

'Nope,' said Dennis. 'The true villain is the
dodgy politician who tried to scam everyone
for his own stinking benefit!

Steam flushed from Wilbur's ears. He

couldn't believe what he was hearing! He'd lost the chance to make more money than he'd ever imagined and been outsmarted by a bunch of kids. Again.

He told Walter to get up and follow him. He was going home to make a video call to his lawyers!

As soon as they'd left, Snooty shared an extra secret.

'Parkinson and I tried for years to get the Beanotown broadband network to be extended out here, but Wilbur would never give permission, because some of the cables needed to be diverted away from his house.

'After he bought Bunkerton, he obviously changed his mind. So the castle now has the strongest signal in town!

'The only catch was there was a three-month waiting list for new cabling, so Wilbur signed a contract agreeing his own private cable could be diverted here instead . . .'

RESULT! Walter and Wilbur were currently Wi-Fi-less! So much for video calling their lawyers online.

'**OOPS!** I don't think Walter will be online playing Fartnite anytime soon!' laughed Dennis.

Pie Face joined in the laughter and clapped a suit of armour on the shoulder, sending it crashing to the ground. A cloud of dust flew up, filling the room, and something started making a very strange sound.

Pie Face shuddered and looked about him through the dust. Was there a werewolf after all? The sound was getting louder . . . And with a deafening roar, the monster became known.

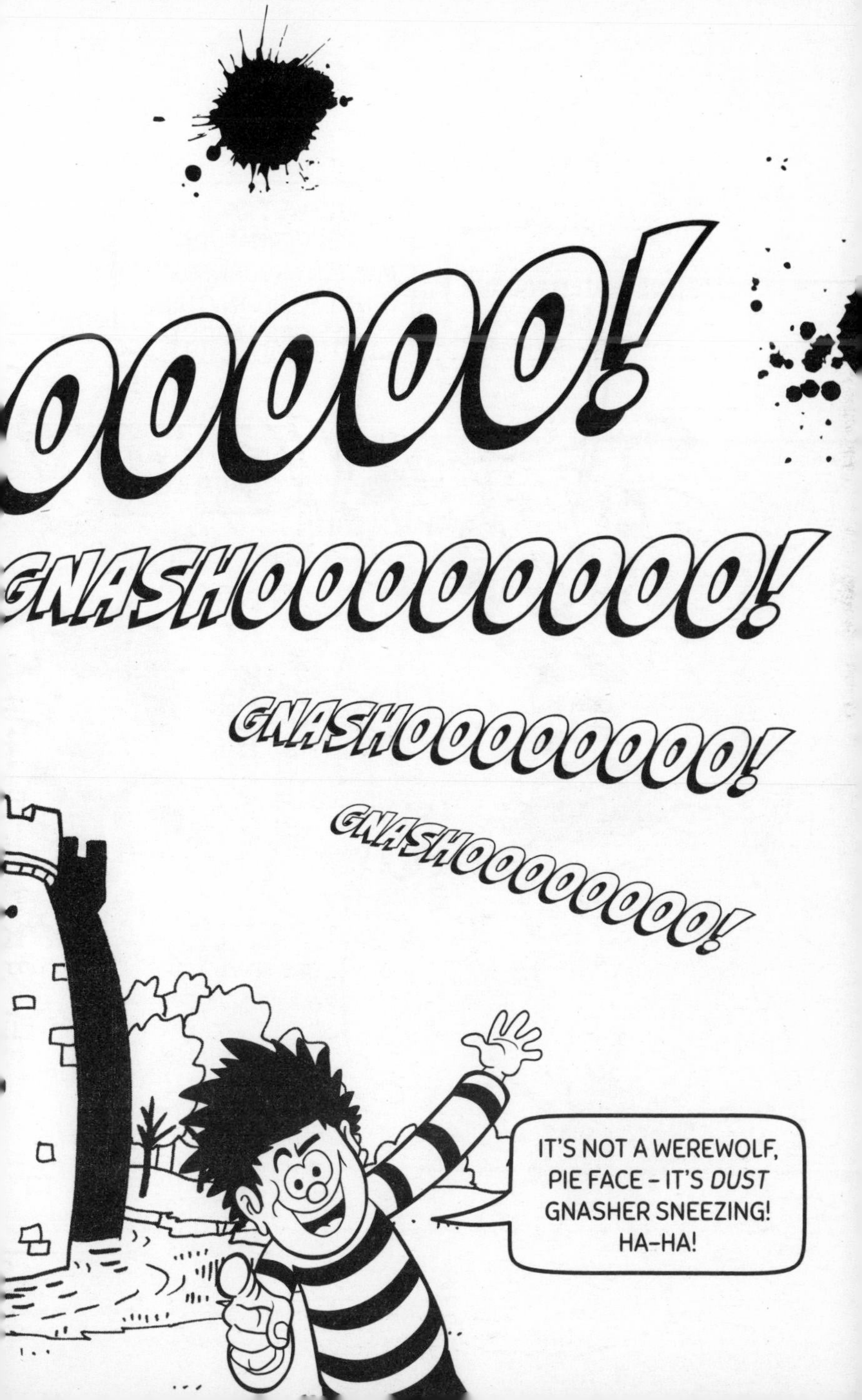

OOOOOO!
GNASHOOOOOOOOO!
GNASHOOOOOOOOO!
GNASHOOOOOOOOO!
IT'S NOT A WEREWOLF, PIE FACE – IT'S *DUST* GNASHER SNEEZING! HA-HA!

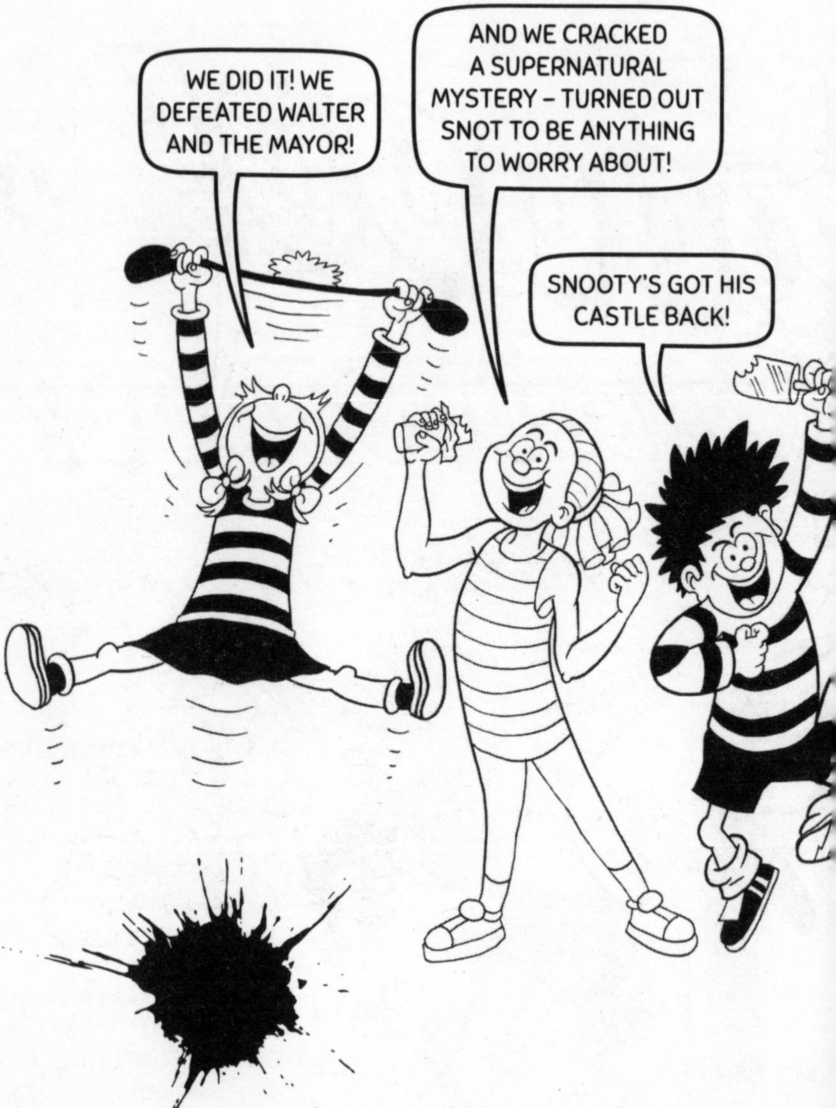
WE DID IT! WE DEFEATED WALTER AND THE MAYOR!
AND WE CRACKED A SUPERNATURAL MYSTERY – TURNED OUT SNOT TO BE ANYTHING TO WORRY ABOUT!
SNOOTY'S GOT HIS CASTLE BACK!

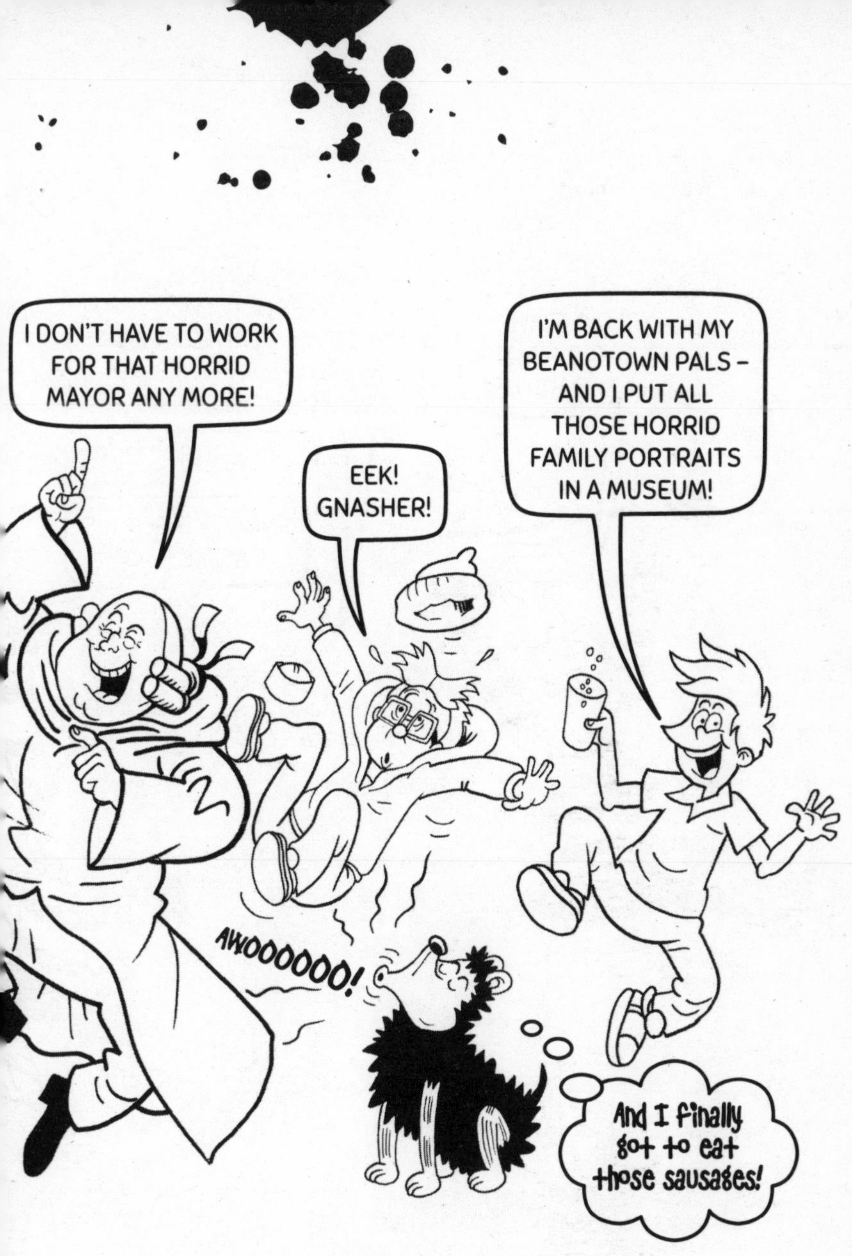
I DON'T HAVE TO WORK FOR THAT HORRID MAYOR ANY MORE!
EEK! GNASHER!
I'M BACK WITH MY BEANOTOWN PALS – AND I PUT ALL THOSE HORRID FAMILY PORTRAITS IN A MUSEUM!
AWOOOOOO!
And I finally got to eat those sausages!

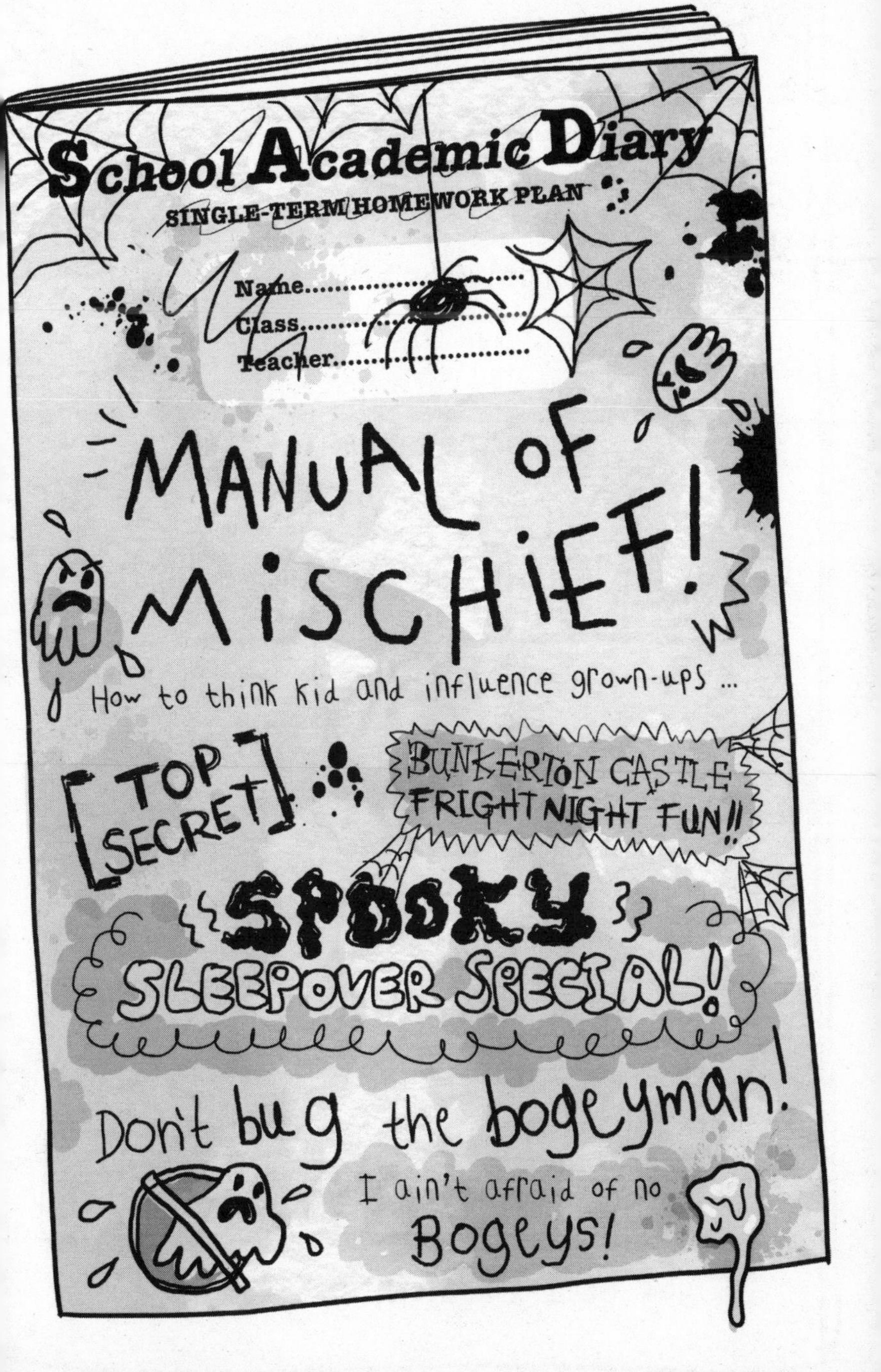
School Academic Diary
SINGLE-TERM HOMEWORK PLAN
Name.......................
Class.......................
Teacher.......................
MANUAL OF MISCHIEF!
How to think kid and influence grown-ups ...
TOP SECRET
BUNKERTON CASTLE FRIGHT NIGHT FUN!!
SPOOKY
SLEEPOVER SPECIAL!
Don't bug the bogeyman!
I ain't afraid of no Bogeys!

When I got invited to a **SPOOKY SLEEPOVER** at Bunkerton Castle, the first thing I thought about was how scared the bogeyman would feel when we rolled up!

YOU were brave enough to finish the whole book, so the reward is a 〰VIP〰 peek into the latest

LEGENDARY

MANUAL OF MISCHIEF !!!

If you've read all I.P. Daley's books, you'll know we stash our secrets inside a bunch of old homework diaries.

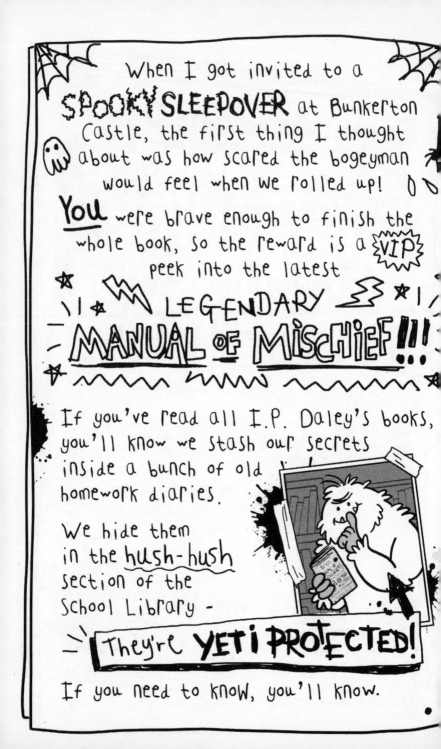

We hide them in the <u>hush-hush</u> section of the school Library -

They're YETI PROTECTED!

If you need to know, you'll know.

AS I always say,

with GREAT PRANKS comes GREAT RESPONSIBILITY

(TO SHARE WITH AS MANY KIDS AS POSSIBLE!)

So next time you forget your homework, just blame it on the bogey!

signed

DENNIS + Gnasher!

P.S. I used to eat my bogeys, but now I just collect them!

WOULD YOU RATHER..?

SPOOKY SLEEPOVER EDITION

JJ is an expert in **CRYPTOZOOLOGY** — the study of creatures that may or may not exist.

BOO!

The bogeyman is believed to be a mythical creature grown-ups invented to scare kids all over the world.

A mythical creature is a supernatural animal, human, or a combination of the two that hasn't been proven to exist in real life.

Shh!

The bogeyman's appearance differs from country to country and even person to person. People who claimed to have seen the bogeyman say they look like whatever you **fear most!**

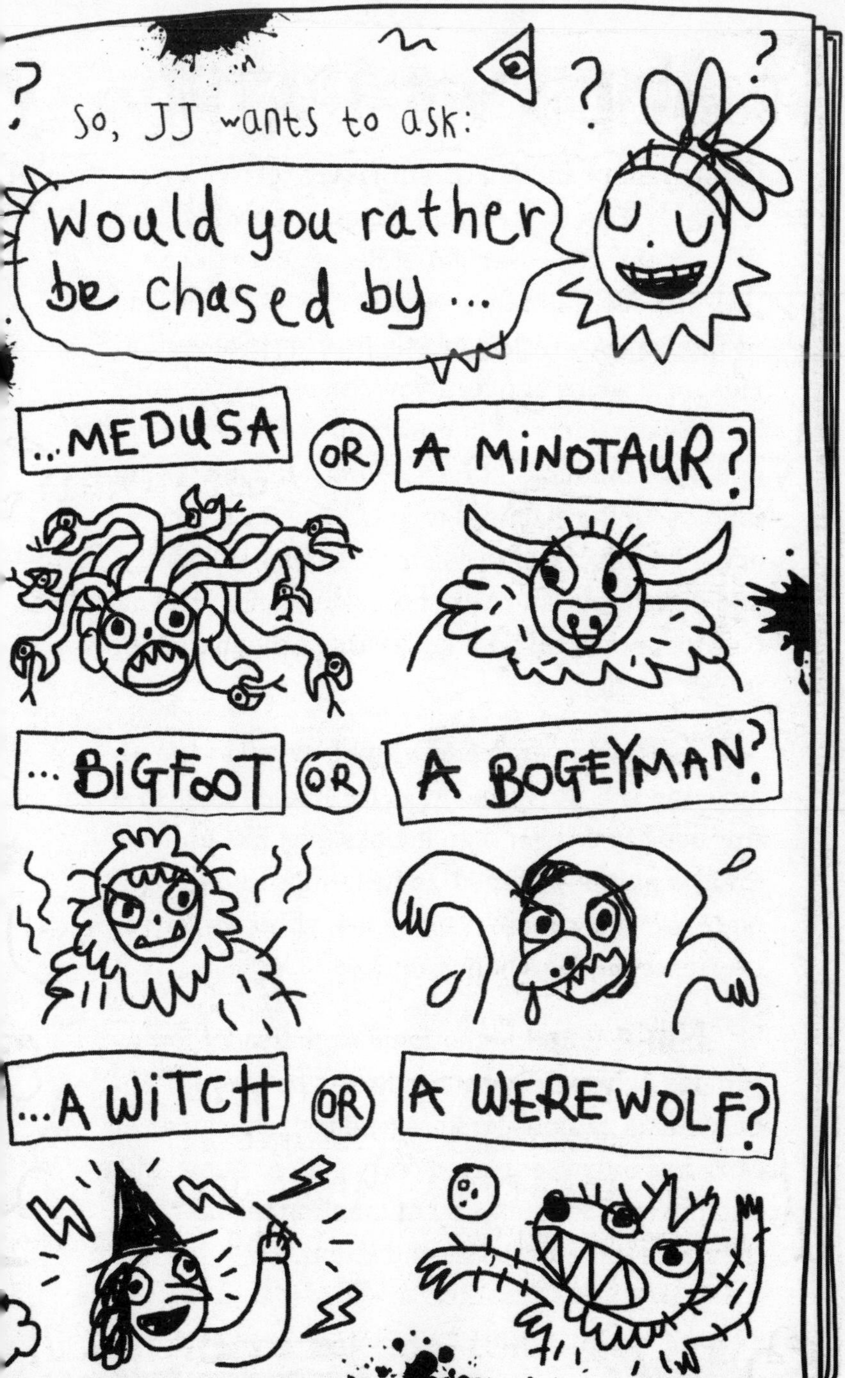
So, JJ wants to ask:
Would you rather be chased by ...
...MEDUSA OR A MINOTAUR?
... BIGFOOT OR A BOGEYMAN?
...A WITCH OR A WEREWOLF?

About the Authors

Craig Graham and Mike Stirling were both born in Kirkcaldy, Fife, in the same vintage year when Dennis first became the cover star of Beano. Ever since, they've been training to become the Brains Behind Beano Books (which is mostly making cool stuff for kids from words and funny pictures). They've both been Beano Editors, but now Craig is Managing Editor and Mike is Editorial Director (ooh, fancy!) at Beano Studios. In the evenings they work for I.P. Daley at her Boomix factory, where Craig fetches coffee and doughnuts, and Mike hoses down her personal bathroom once an hour (at least). It's the ultimate Beano mission!

Craig lives in Fife with his wife Laura and amazing kids Daisy and Jude. He studied English so this book is smarter than it looks (just like him). Craig is partially sighted, so he bumps into things quite a lot. He couldn't be happier, although fewer bruises would be a bonus.

Mike is an International Ambassador for Dundee (where Beano started!) and he lives in Carnoustie, famous for its legendary golf course. Mike has only ever played crazy golf. At home, Mike and his wife Sam relax by untangling the hair of their adorable kids, Jessie and Elliott.